The Bishop Brothers:

In Love with the Same Girl

Author Shortee

TYANNA PRESENTS

Synopsis

All was well in Cornell "C-Note" Bishop's life. He had a loving fiancée and a thriving illegal drug business. That changed the moment his fiancée was killed by the police, followed by him being setup and sentenced to five years in prison. Upon his release, Cornell sets his plans in motion: seek revenge against his brother and reclaim the street throne, which was once his.

Cortez Bishop had the life he longed for. His brother behind bars, street clout, and a woman he could care less for. Yearning to happily live as the street king he had become, Cortez's world explodes into chaos. Within a blink of an eye, Cortez began to recognize his wrongs and fight for the one person he really needs- his woman, Tonia.

Tonia hadn't had the best relationship with Cortez, yet she loved him unconditionally. That was until trials and tribulations pushed her into the open, sincere, and loving arms of another man. Confused and afraid, Tonia is placed in a whirlwind of disarray as she badly wants to follow her heart, even though her mind speaks differently.

Will Cornell reclaim his throne? What will become of Cornell and Cortez? Who will Tonia choose Cortez or Cornell?

Acknowledgments

I wanna thank God for giving me this wonderful gift of writing...

Now first and foremost, I want to thank my husband, Eddie, who is my #1 fan. Thank you, babe, for rocking with me and supporting me when I told you I wanted to be a writer.

To my babies, Eddie IV, Deandre, and Lakiaya, Mama loves the three of you so much. I'm doing this for y'all so you will know you can always follow your dreams

Mama, thank you for believing in me and supporting me. Who would have thought that I would be an author, right? But you supported me through it all. You have bought and read every book I have written, and that means a lot.

Pops, thanks for your support as well. I am hoping and praying that you will be back home soon instead of being behind those walls where you don't belong #freemypops.

I love you, old man.

Sis, Cassie, I love you, girl. You are a strong woman. Thanks for your support. To all six of my nieces and nephews: Destiny, Damarion, Dominic, Izaiah, and Serenity. Let's not forget the new member of our family, Hakai. I love all six of y'all.

To my cuzzos: Hallee and Lexee, thank you for y'all support we rocking 'til the wheels fall off. no doubt. I love you and my little cousins, all six of them.

Lora, you have told me time and time again that you made a promise to me when I was younger that you will always be there for me, and you have stuck by that promise. Thank you for the support as well. It does mean a lot.

Chey, Phylicia, and Lonzia, you three have been there for me from the jump. When I wanted to quit, y'all pushed me not to. And y'all have become like family to me, and I love y'all for that.

Zhakirah, thank you for supporting me, sis. You know how I'm coming no doubt.

Amanda, Shae, and Sweets, thank y'all for rocking with me as well. Also for supporting me, y'all are the best.

Tyanna and the whole Tyanna Presents family, thank y'all for even accepting me. Y'all all made me feel welcomed. Including you, TN Jones. You make my day.

Dedication

R.I.P Grandpa Richard. #fuckcancer.

Mama Diane, we miss you, we love you and will see you soon.

Uncle Frank, we miss you so much, and love you.

Prologue

Cornell

Five years ago...

I was riding my brother around the town and we were kicking it. I was getting married tomorrow to the love of my life, Stacee, so we were hopping from bar to bar. One bar we went to, we were having so much fun. This badass bitch was dancing all over us, but my brother, Cortez, was feeling her more than any of us. Shit, she was a bad bitch. If I wasn't getting married tomorrow, I would have been fucking her ass in the bathroom. Yeah, I didn't have respect for these bitches out here. She was dancing on this random ass nigga that came up in our section, but I don't even know how he even got in our area anyway. My brother Cortez got mad when he saw dude pull out his dick, getting ready to fuck her in the club. It ain't like my brother never done no shit like that before, but baby girl was drunk. So, she wasn't aware of what was going on.

"Nigga, if you don't get your ugly duckling looking ass up out my section, trying to fuck my girl! How the fuck you in here trying to fuck baby girl and she all drunk? What are you a fucking rapist? You know she doesn't have a clue what the fuck is going on! I should beat the shit out of your ol' weekend lover ass."

I just shook my head at this dumb ass nigga. This nigga must be deaf or something 'cause he still was trying to fuck this bitch. He starts rubbing his dick on her pussy, and that really pissed my brother off, but ol' girl didn't move either. She was just grinding on his dick as they sat on the couch across from us. It must have slipped in 'cause she popped her eyes open fast as hell and tried to hop up, but he snatched her ass by the throat. That there alarmed me. This nigga was going to rape shawty, so I hopped up along with my brother. We stomped our way over to Lil' mama, and this cat, and I pulled my strap out.

"Yo, my nigga, I would advise you to let her go right now or I'ma put two to your head. What's it going to be?"

This nigga looked like he wasn't fazed by us both having our guns on 'em. See, we weren't your average dope boys. We were rich off of trust funds, so we had to stay strapped up just in case. Well, that just in case moment has surfaced right now. He started fucking this girl like she was his bitch, and that pissed me off. He was sitting here raping this girl after she told him to stop and tried to hop off his lap, but he snatched her ass back. She had tears in her eyes and was scared. My brother was on one end and I was on the other. I put my gun to his head and my brother put his on the other side. We both pulled the trigger at the same time, and the nigga was dead instantly.

Lil' mama starting screaming, so I bent down and whispered in her ear, "Look, Ma, quit screaming before you draw attention to us. I'm going to get his body out of here, but you need to hop off his dick right now."

She hurried and hopped up and pulled her skirt down. I could see her pretty pussy, and I knew I was going to have to have her eventually. "What's your name, Ma?"

"I—I—I'm Tonia Keys. What's your name?" She was stuttering. I knew she was scared, but she had nothing to be scared of. We wasn't going to hurt her; we were protecting her.

"Well, I'm Cornell, and this here is my little brother Cortez. We aren't going to hurt you. We are actually protecting you; that's how we were raised."

She looked down, and I hated that I had her nervous, but fuck it. I couldn't worry about that right now. I had to think fast on how to get this body out of the club. Thank God we were in the back. This was where we loved to be every time we came here to take the attention off us. Being the Bishop brothers always drew attention. I saw our boy Smurf walk up and his was timing was everything.

"Yo bro, we just bodied that nigga over there. Do you think ya boys can ease him out the back entrance

and handle that body? The price will be right and in your account in twenty minutes."

Smurf nodded his head and no words were spoken. He handled it. We went back to partying as if nothing ever happened, and the chick that I now knew as Tonia came and sat next to me.

She placed her head on my shoulder. "Thank you for what you have done for me."

"No problem, Ma, but look, you can't be laying your head on my shoulder like that. You will have people thinking that we hooking up when I can't have that I'm getting married tomorrow."

"Shit, we can hook up just for tonight and act like it never happened though."

"Naw, I'm good. I ain't fucking up my happy home for some random." I looked over, and my brother was mugging me, but I didn't want this bitch. He can have her ass. "Check this, Ma. Why don't you holler at my brother right there looking over here? He is feeling you way more than I am anyway."

"Nigga, fuck you then. I don't want your little dick ass anyway. I was just showing gratitude for saving me!"

She got up and stormed off towards my brother. I looked at my Rolex and shook my head at the time. I needed to get my black ass home. So I headed over to my brother to tell him I was out. "Look, bro. I'm about to get outta here. You riding out or you staying?"

Before he answered me, he turned to the chick, Tonia. "Ma, you coming with me or what?" He questioned.

I looked at the chick because his ass was taking too long to answer me. Shit, if she wanted to be a hoe and go home with him, that was her business. It ain't got shit to do with me. I just hope she cleans that thing first before she let my brother run-up in it. She had finally nodded her head, yes, letting him know she was down.

"Well, let's go then. I need to get me some rest before my wedding." I dapped up all the homies and we all walked out of the bar, hopping in my 1995

Chevy Impala SS. I sped off towards my brother's crib to drop them off. It took me about ten minutes to reach his spot. They climbed out of my car. "Aiight, bruh, I will see you at about eleven o'clock tomorrow." I sped off as they walked towards the door.

I was driving about ten minutes when I noticed that the cops were behind me, pulling me over. I rolled my window down and had my hands on the steering wheel, because we all know how these damn pigs be these days. They will find any reason to shoot you. The officer walked over to my car.

"Do you know why I pulled your ass over?"

"Hell, I'm sorry. I mean, no, I don't. Why did you pull me over, officer?"

"Well, you were doing sixty in a thirty-five lane. May I have your license and registration."

I reached into my glove box, handed him the necessary paperwork, and he turned, walking back to his car. I picked up my phone and created a group message for me, Stacee, and Cortez.

Me: *Police just pulled me over. He said I was doing 60 in a 35. I feel like he on some bs, so I'm on 71 highway past 59th St. So get here now.*

I sat and waited. My phone went off, and the officer still wasn't on his way to my car yet.

Stacee: *Wtf?! I'm on the way.*

Cortez: *Man, wtf?! I can't get to you. You know shawty here and I'm drunk.*

See, that's the thing about my brother that I hated. I could be there for him when he needed me, but when it comes to me, he couldn't do the same for me.

Me: *Whatever, Cortez. I'm sick of your ass always wanting me there for you, and you can't be there for me.*

I blocked his number and waited for this punk ass officer to come back to my car. As soon as he was headed over to me, Stacee pulled up. Thank God she did too. I looked over, and she hopped out the car 'cause she must have felt what I felt too.

"Can you step out the car, sir?"

I stepped out the car as he asked me to. "What did I do, officer?"

"*Well, it says you are wanted in a shooting that happened at the bar tonight. I'm going to have to search your car.*"

I was shocked as fuck at what he was saying because nobody saw what happened but those that were in the section with us. And I know they ain't talking 'cause they are street niggas, and they don't fuck with the boys.

"*Cornell, what is going on. baby?*"

"*Ma'am, I'm going to ask you to step back, please.*"

He had his hand on his gun. I knew he was about to really be on some bullshit, but I knew that Stacee wasn't going to back down either. I was praying that things didn't turn worse than I thought.

"*I'm not going anywhere, that is my fiancé, and you're not about to do him like y'all do every other African American man.*"

"*I'm not gonna tell you again to get the fuck back. *"

Next thing I know, the officer was letting off shots into my fiancée, and I was kneeling on the ground, holding her head in my arms.

"*I was going to tell you I'm pregnant.*"

That was the last thing she said before I lost it on the officer. He killed my baby and my fiancée and he was going to pay.

"No, wait! I know who sent me to pull you over."

"Then speak, muthafucka."

He started to stutter, "I--I—It was somebody named Cortez."

I couldn't believe what he just said to me. My own brother set me up, and now my wife and child are dead. I walked over and punched the officer in the face, and that was it. Yep, I got them muthafucking hands. Them one hitta quitta's, baby. I walked over to my girl, picked her head up, and just held her head in my lap, crying. I couldn't believe my baby was gone, and it all had something to do with my punk-ass brother, Cortez. I'mma get that nigga for what he did. I picked up my phone, called my brother and got no answer. Should have known to him its pussy over bros. I just couldn't get down with that anymore.

So I just picked her up and left that officer on the ground. Shit, fuck that nigga. He killed my family, so I don't give a fuck what happens to him now. I walked over, placed her limp body in the back of my car. I hopped in the front and took my baby to the hospital. What was supposed to be a ten to fifteen drive, I turned into five minutes. Pulling up into the emergency parking lot, I hopped out the car, opened the back door, got my girl out, and ran into the hospital.

"P—p—please somebody help! My girl was shot and she's pregnant!"

A nurse ran up to me with a gurney and I laid my wife's lifeless body on the gurney.

"Ok, sir, I will be right back with you. Sit here and wait."

I knew that she was gone already, but I couldn't bring myself to say anything right now. The only thing that was on my mind is paying Cortez back for what he caused today. I lost my wife and child all at once. As I was sitting there waiting for the doctor or nurse to come out to tell me what I already knew, an officer walked up to me.

"Are you Cordell Bishop?"

"Yeah. Who wants to know and why?"

"KCPD. We are here to question you about an assault on an officer tonight."

"Well, y'all might as well have a seat 'cause I'm not going anywhere till I find out if my girl will be ok."

"Oh, see, we can question you right here. We don't need to go downtown right now."

I knew I was about to end up in jail that night, but shit, I didn't give a fuck. I was protecting my wife.

"So, an officer identified you as his attacker. Would you like to tell us why you attacked the officer?"

"Well, since he identified me, let me tell you what happened. He pulled me over saying I was speeding, but I know I wasn't. Anyway, I gave him a copy of my license, registration, and proof of insurance. While he was in his car, I hit my fiancée up and told her what was going on and she told me she was on the way. I was only five minutes away from my house. Well, soon as the officer was headed back to my car, she pulled up. She was asking him what was going on, but he had already told me to get out my car because he had to search it. He wouldn't tell me what for or even tell her. Then next thing I know, he was telling her to get the fuck back to her car. So she goes on and tells him she ain't leaving her fiancée. Next thing I know, he raises his gun to let off shots into my wife. And yeah, I was pissed off and snapped on his ass. I only hit him one time, but he shot my wife, and she is pregnant. If she dies, he will get away with it."

After I spoke my peace, a doctor came out and asked for the family of Stacee Hayes. I hopped up and walked over to the doctor.

"I'm her fiancé. How is she? Can I see her?"

"Well sir, we did everything we could to save her, but she was dead upon arrival. She sustained a GSW to the chest that pierced her heart. She and the baby did not make it."

I dropped to my knees and just cried for my fiancé and child. This officer killed my fiancé and child, and my own punk-ass brother was behind me getting pulled over. e reason I lost my girl in the first place and he was gonna pay.

Chapter 1
Cornell

I was sitting in my cell, just thinking about how I can't wait to get revenge on Cortez for him not being there after he set me up. See, what he doesn't know is his girl has been coming to see me every week, and I was about to make her mine. She was starting to fall for me, and I could tell, but I wasn't feeling her like that just yet. She was just a part of the plan.

Oh shit, where are my manners? I haven't introduced myself. Well, my name is Cornell, but my peoples call me C-Note. I was born and raised here in Kansas City, Mo (The Show-me State). My mother was a single parent raising me and my brother, Cortez on her own. Our father left her after we were born. That deadbeat ass nigga didn't even stay long. He saw us being born and that was that. He dipped off right after and never looked back. Fuck that nigga, though.

This ain't about him. This is about me going after my brother. So back to me, I'm thirty years old, about six-foot-one, with dreads, and I have a few tattoos and a six-pack. I'm what these women call a snack out here. I have some jewelry I like to wear, but me being in this damn jail cell, I can't. My day is coming soon.

Three years ago, I was calling my brother's phone, but as usual, he didn't answer. I called his phone again, but this time Tonia answered and said that my brother left his phone at their house. We talked for a good minute then she gave me her number. From that day on, we had been talking and writing letters, or she would come visit me. Those visits were everything to me. Shit, I still tried to call my brother, but each time he didn't answer the phone. So when he didn't answer, I would call her and we would talk. The last time that I called her, she told me that she couldn't wait till I got to come home. We have been waiting on this day for a long time. All these visits, calls, and letters were doing something to me, and I was beginning to fall for her. I wasn't supposed to fall for her. She was only supposed to be part of the plan to go after my brother for payback, but she didn't know that, and I wanted to keep it that way. But these feelings just kept getting deeper and deeper.

I felt like shit because I was supposed to love Stacee forever, but I can't keep loving a ghost. I had to let her go. And what better way than to go after the people who had something to do with her and my child not being here. If I knew this woman, I knew she was ready to take things to the next level. Her dating my brother didn't mean shit to me. At this point, I wanted to be happy, and she makes me happy. Tonia told me her hope and dreams in our visits. She wants to get married and have kids, but she also wanted to open her own Tattoo shop that my brother didn't want to help her with. He wanted her to stay home and do nothing but spend his money. I want her to have her own money and not depend on mine for nothing. I want her to better herself. Her telling me that my brother didn't want to invest in her future kinda threw me off and made me want to help her with opening her shop.

The night that Stacee getting killed, I ended up being charged with the assault on a police officer, but they left out the murder in the club that night cause they knew that they didn't have shit. I pled guilty for the assault on that officer and ended up doing 5 years behind it. The officer that killed my wife got off with murder. My time was almost up, and everybody that harmed me in some type away before I got locked up or let's just say the ones that are the reason I'm here was going to have hell to pay when I come home. Nobody knew I was getting out next week, and it was going to stay that way for now.

Chapter 2

Cortez

Let me introduce myself. I am Cortez Bishop, the little brother of Cornell Bishop, and I have always been jealous of my brother. He was always the favorite and the chosen one, while I was the screw-up in my family... until I got the idea to have that nigga locked up for a crime he didn't commit. But the officer I sent after him didn't just do that. He killed my brother's fiancée, which he wasn't supposed to. He was only supposed to arrest him for the drugs I planted in his trunk, but he never got that far because Stacee little annoying ass showed up, wouldn't fucking leave, and the cop on the job ended up killing her stupid ass. Shit, how was I supposed to know she was pregnant, and she wouldn't leave? But oh fucking well. That night I met my now fiancée, Tonia Keys. She is the love of my life at least that's how I feel. I've wanted her since the first night we met. That night I brought her home with me, and we have been together since she gave me that phat juicy pussy.

I'm twenty-five years old. I'm about five foot eight, weighing one-hundred and eighty pounds. I work out on an everyday basis. People say I look a lot like Lance Gross, so I must be sexy as hell. Shit, y'all know what I look like. I don't even need to explain how sexy I am for y'all to know. Just know I'm a sexy beast.

Getting up out the bed, I went and hopped in the shower so I could get ready for work. See, I am a music producer and own my own company that I started with the money I made from selling drugs. I was trying to get it by any means necessary since my mother cut me off after finding out I was with Tonia instead of helping Cornell. I don't even know how she found out because far as I knew, my brother didn't tell her what went down. I didn't know who else could have mentioned it since Stacee isn't here to speak. I could be mistaken though, but I don't know. I sure was going to figure it out one way or another.

Stepping out the shower after washing up, I grabbed my towel, wrapped it around my waist, and walked out the bathroom into my room. Not paying attention, I walked right into Tonia, who was rocking this little outfit that had her body looking right and nice as fuck.

"Hey, baby. Where you headed to? "

"Hey, Ma. I'm actually headed to look over these papers at the office."

"Ok. Well, I was hoping you would come to the prison to visit your brother with me."

"Naw, Ma, y'all can have that. I don't wanna see that nigga and you know that."

"I don't understand what has gotten into you lately, but your hate for your brother is gotten worse over the last five years. Why do you hate your brother so much?"

This is the shit I'm talking about with her. She was always having this nigga's back like they were in a relationship. But I wasn't about to go there with her today.

"Look, Ma. I'm not about to do this back and forth with you today, so please just let it go."

I turned, walked into my walk-in closet, and found me something to wear today. After throwing on my clothes, I grabbed my keys off the counter, walked out the door, jumped in my car, and sped the fuck off. I pulled up to my studio in no time.

I went inside and headed right to my office that I had here in the studio. Sitting down at my desk, I began to go over this paperwork, but as I was, I got to thinking about how much I hated my brother. Since we were kids, my mother always favored him more. I could never do anything right in her eyes. So that and the way he acted in the club that night, pushed me into having that officer arrest his ass five years ago.

And I felt nothing about what took place.

Like I said, I gave no fucks. See, I was now this big ass producer and my brother wasn't shit. I was living my best life and getting ready to get married in just two months to the love of my life.

The ringing of my office phone brought me out my little daydream.

"Hello, babe. I'm here with your mother and Cornell. He's getting out today! Well, he is out already, but he needs a place to stay."

"Ok, what are you telling me for?"

"I'm telling you because nigga, your brother is coming to stay with us."

"No the fuck he isn't! You don't make decisions on your own! You talk to me first!"

He must have taken the phone from her. "Hey, lil' bro. You need to chill out. I'm coming to stay with you and that's final. Quit talking to your girl like you controlling her."

"Nigga, whatever. Fuck you."

I hung up the phone and got pissed off about this whole situation. Getting up out my office, I had to take a drive because I just couldn't deal with this shit right now. I have plans and I know if anything, my brother is going to fuck up them up. If I know anything about my brother, he wasn't going to let go of him going to jail or his bitch getting killed while she was pregnant with his kid. He's going to want to know why he went to jail. Pulling up to my destination, I jumped out the car. Knocking on the door, I waited for the person I came to see to open the damn door.

"Who the fuck is it?"

"It's Cortez! Open the damn door before someone sees me out here."

"Man, what the fuck are you doing here?" Officer Jeremy Rodgers asked.

"Look, man. Cornell is out, so you gonna have to watch your back. I'm sure he is gonna come after you for killing his fiancée."

"I knew that day would finally come, but I didn't think that it would be so soon."

"You better either leave town or go into hiding 'cause he's coming, and he will be coming for revenge."

"Fuck! Fuck! Fuck! I guess I will pack me and my family up to leave town."

I nodded my head then turned to walk out of the house. Jumping back into the car, I pulled off with no destination in mind and just drove around to clear my mind.

29

Chapter 3

Tonia

After Cornell hung up with Cortez, we all headed out the jail towards my car. We were headed to drop his mom off first then to go shopping so he could get clothes and shoes. This was the happiest day of my life. I can't believe my baby was finally coming home. I know what y'all are thinking, but shit, I wanted Cornell since day one. I just settled for Cortez because Cornell was getting married and wouldn't give me the time of day back then. However, the tragic death of his fiancée brought us closer. We have been fucking around now for three years. At first, it started out with me just talking to him over the phone, then it went to me visiting him and us also writing letters to each other. When I would go visit, we would laugh and just really get to know each other more. I thought that maybe it was because Cortez wasn't giving me the time

I needed, but I also found out that he was cheating. I started falling for Cornell extra hard around that time, but as I stated before, I was already feeling him way before. That night Cornell saved me from being raped in the club five years ago; he was my knight in shining armor.

Him losing his fiancée was very tragic, and I was there for him in his time of need, so maybe that's why he came on to me at one of his visits three years ago. Things have been easy to hide from Cortez, but now that Cornell was getting out, it would be harder now that he will be living with us. I don't even love Cortez at all. I am in love with Cornell. I just hope he felt the same way as me or this all would be for nothing.

Oh shit! My name is Tonia Keys, and I am twenty-nine years old, five foot seven, weighing about one hundred and fifty pounds with caramel skin tone. Most say I look like Lyrica from Love and Hip hop. I loved the skin I am in for sure.

Now let's get back on the topic at hand; the two brothers that I am dealing with at this moment. One is dangerous and the other, not so dangerous... so I thought. I have been trying to get my dancing career off since I could remember. I've done music videos, and I've also stripped too, but I only do that when I need the money, and I haven't been getting any dancing gig.

See, before I met Cornell and Cortez, I was stripping here and there. I was already in multiple music videos, but just after me and Cortez started dating, things went downhill. He always wanted me at home. He never wanted me to do my music videos or strip, but that's how I made my money. I was all about getting to that bag by any means necessary. Even if that meant that me and Cortez will not be an us any longer, but shit, what did I care for? I wasn't really in love with him; I am in love with his brother.

Pulling up to my house, I got out the car with Cornell following behind me. I was ready to feel that dick inside me. He had been talking freaky to me the whole way to the Legends, then after the Legends, he was back on his shit being freaky. Rushing into the house, he followed me to the room that we were to have him in. Soon as we got into the room, we closed the door began kissing each other like it was our last time. Pulling his shirt over his head and then his pants and boxers off, I dropped to my knees and began to suck the fuck outta his long thick pole he had between his legs.

"Awww fuck, girl! Suck this dick, girl."

I did just that. I started to deep throat his dick to where I felt him touching my tonsils, but shit, I had no gag reflex, so I wouldn't choke. Soon as his dick hit the back of my throat, he released down my throat and I swallowed every bit of it. He looked down at me, biting his lip. He pulled me up and laid me down on the bed, removing my pants and thongs. I took off my shirt and bra as he dipped down and started kissing my inner thighs. Every kiss was getting to me and had me anticipating what was getting ready to happen. He kissed my lips then began to suck on my clit; that shit was feeling so amazing. I haven't ever felt like this, not even with his brother.

"Aww, shit! Yesss, baby! Fuck, I'm bout to cum!"

"Let that shit go, baby. Let me taste your nectar, mama."

He didn't have to tell me twice, I released all that has been building up. This man was doing something to my body that has never been done, and I was here for it for damn sure. He rose up and hovered over me, rubbing his dick over my clit. Then he eased the head in. Oh my god, that shit felt amazing. He pushed himself in further until he was all the way in. I felt pain and pleasure all at once, and it felt so good right. He was serving those long, deep strokes, making me cum in no time.

"Awww shit, mama. Your pussy is so tight and wet. You gonna make me cum too soon and I ain't tryna cum yet. Come ride this dick."

He pulled out, laid back on the bed, and I hopped on his dick. I began to ride him nice and slow. I was riding him as if my life depended on it. Slowly, I lifted up then slowly back down. His eyes began to roll in the back of his head. I leaned back and began to massage his balls. Then the next thing I know, I felt his balls tighten up in my hands, so I began to speed up. As I sped up, I was cumming and released all over his shaft.

"Aww, fuck, daddy! I'm cumming.!"

"Shit! Me too, ma. Me too."

We both released. After I rolled off him, lying next to him to catch my breath. As he looked at me, the look in his eyes looked like love, but I didn't want to be wrong about what was in his eyes.

"Babe, can we talk right quick before we get up and wash up?" Cornell asked.

"Sure, what's on your mind?"

"So we been seeing each other for what three years now, right?"

"Yeah, that's right, babe."

"Well, I wanna know how you really feel about me. If you are all on like I am because I have fallen for you when I shouldn't have. You are my brother's fiancée. Even though that nigga is a grimy ass nigga, I still feel bad about what we are doing. But I have fallen for you, so I'm saying all this to tell you that I think I've fallen in love with you."

"Cornell, baby, I'm all in, and I love you too. You came into my life in a time that I needed someone in my corner. You saved me all those years ago from that guy that was trying to rape me. I thought that we would never get this chance, but for unfortunate reasons, you are now in my life, and I couldn't be happier. Yeah, I'm with your brother, but I don't love him like I love you. To tell you the truth, I don't love your brother at all and never have. He doesn't believe in me like you do."

"What happened to Stacee hurt me so much, but I found you. That I can be happy about but my brother, I can't say the same. At this point, me and my brother are not on the same page like we used to be, so I can't think about how he feels. I'm in love and I am happy. I haven't been happy like this in a long time since Stacee."

I nodded then got up to go take a shower. As I was getting in the shower, I felt the cold air from the shower door being opened. I turned around, and Cornell was climbing in the shower with me. I wrapped my arms around his neck and stepped on my tippy toes to kiss his lips, but he took it much further. This nigga wanted to go for another round and I was all for it right now. I couldn't get enough of his ass right now anyway. I didn't care that we were in the home that I shared with Cortez right now. I loved the thrill of possibly getting caught.

He lifted me in the air and began to eat my box. He was going to town on this pussy. I never had this feeling ever before. He was licking from front to back and had me cumming in no time. After cumming, he lowered me down, so I lowered myself to my knees and took his tool in my mouth. I made sure to lick the head before I began to take him in my mouth.

He started to grip my hair and fuck my face. His dick was hitting the back of my throat, and two strokes later, he was releasing down my throat. Standing up, he lifted me, and I wrapped my legs around his body as he placed the head of his dick at my opening and pushed his way inside. Soon as I felt that big thick dick fill me up, it felt amazing. I started bouncing on his dick, stepped out of the shower, and took me to the room, lying me on the bed.

He spread my legs wide open and then began to pound my pussy. He was putting a hurting on my kitty while rubbing on my clit.

"Oh fuck! I'm cumming, baby."

"Shit, let that shit go. I'm cumming with you, baby."

We both came hard as fuck. He rolled off me and laid there breathing hard as hell, trying to catch his breath. Meanwhile, I laid there staring up at the ceiling, thinking of what I would have to do to end things with Cortez but couldn't come up with anything at this point, so I curled up under Cornell and fell fast asleep.

Chapter 4

Cornell

Yo boy is finally home and I am happy to be out. Now its time for me to get my plan in motion and get back to the streets. I was ready to take back over my spot that I was supposed to have anyway. Me being sent away for those five years fucked me up, but now it was time for me to come back and get revenge on those that had something to do with me going down and for Stacee not being here. That officer that killed her, Officer Jeremy was going to pay and what way for him to pay is with his life. Now, my brother, I can't kill him, but I was going to take his girl from him and then make him regret ever fucking wit' me tryna get me for that murder. I knew didn't anybody find that body 'cause the homies disposed of that body. That's why that shit wasn't on my paperwork. Laying back in the bed, I wrapped my arms around Tonia and fell asleep right along with her.

Later that evening...

I was in the shower getting ready to hit these streets; it's time for me to go meet the homies. Cortez thinking he still that nigga, but he won't be for long. I heard he more at that label then handling these streets, so this will be like taking candy from a baby. Getting out the shower, I walked in the room, and this nigga Cortez was walking around, looking through my shit.

"Nigga, can I help you with something? Why you going through my shit like it's yours?

"Nigga, I bought this shit, Cuz. The fuck you mean?"

"Cuz you ain't bought shit I got in these here bags you can kick rocks bitch."

"We will see, bitch."

He turned and walked out of the room while I continued to get dressed. I don't know what this fool was up to, but I sure was going to find out. But I know one thing he wasn't gonna send me back to jail. I needed to go get my dreads retwisted, so I was about to hit the homegirl Liz up; she be doing that dope shit I heard. I would hit her soon as I finished handling the business in the streets. That's number one right now, nothing before these streets. Walking out the room, I went to find Tonia to see if I can borrow her car 'til I can get my SS out of the shop I had it in. Yeah, I was ready to ride out in my 95 impala SS. I was getting it painted candy red that mothafucka was gonna be dope.

"Aye Tonia, can I use your car to run a few errands and go get my hair done? I should be back in a few hours."

"Yeah, go ahead. No problem, bro. By the time you come back, dinner should be ready." She turned to my brother.

"Cortez sweetheart, are you 'bout to head out or are you staying home with me?"

"Aiight, I'm out. I will holla at you two later when I get back."

"I'm headed back to the label then to check on the streets and make sure these niggas are on they shit like they suppose to. I will see you later."

I heard something that sounded like a kiss, but I had already turned to go grab her keys off the key holder they had hung by the door. Getting in the car, I hurried and sped off before I saw my brother come out. Pulling down the street, I watched as my brother pulled out the driveway then headed in the opposite direction, so I followed behind him. I wanted to see what this nigga was up to first. See, Tonia told me all about this nigga cheating on her. She said she confronted this nigga, and he cut the chick off, but we will see when he gets to his destination. He was in a residential area, not no shit like a record label like he was supposed to be going to. Watching him pull up to a house, I parked down the street where he couldn't see me as I watched him go up to the door and place his key in. Soon as the door opened, what I saw next was a shocker to me. I thought this bitch left years ago when we chased her out of town.

See, some odd years back, before I even did my time, we were hitting these streets hard. When I first started fucking with Stacee, I was also fucking with this chick named Sarah. She was a white bitch that I met while being at the club one night. We hit it off well when she came up into our VIP section. I took her to my hideaway spot that I took all chicks, that weren't wifey, too. That night we fucked all over the spot, and we had fucked almost every day after... 'til she caught feelings and got pregnant. She didn't want to get rid of the baby 'til I forced her ass to. After she had the abortion, she tried threatening me that she was going to tell Stacee about our affair, so I paid her ass off, told her ass to leave and never look back.

Here I am looking at this snake ass bitch kissing my brother like they were in love or some shit. Then what I saw next was a complete shocker. Here I was staring at a little boy that looked like he was about four or five. I just shook my head then hit reverse down the street. I don't know how I was going to tell Tonia that this nigga had a whole family with another bitch. I don't know if I want to tell her who it is or not.

Both these mothafuckas are snakes. I don't know how long they been fucking around, but that kid sure looks like my brother. He could have been seeing this bitch since he got with Tonia, but I sure was going to find out. I just had to keep watching this nigga. Pulling up to the hood, I saw my niggas, Red and Preston. These were my niggas right here. They been watching my brother for me while I was gone and keeping me up on game. Parking the car, I hopped out, and these niggas pulled on me. I just laughed at these niggas and put my hands up.

"Say, Cuz, it's me C-Note. Put the damn guns down."

They lowered their guns, walked over to me, and dapped me up. We walked into the house, taking a seat at the table. We sat and chopped it up for a minute, catching up on what's been going on. They told me my dumb ass brother been telling these niggas not to give me any information whatsoever about the trap business. But these fools weren't following his orders. They were on my side anyway, so we were 'bout to take this shit over. We sat and chopped it up a little longer then I headed out. Now it was time for me to head over to Liz's crib to get my hair done. I sped off towards Liz's place out south. It took me a good fifteen minutes to get there. Hopping out my ride after parking in her driveway, I knocked on her door.

"Who the fuck is it?"

"It's C-Note, Ma."

She swung the door open. "Nigga, when you get home. Ugh, why you dreads look nappy like that nigga in Kansas Nappy dreads? Get your ass in here so we can fix you up right we can't have you out here looking like Nappy dreads bro."

"I just got out this morning; I been away for five years. Shit, I wasn't letting none of them niggas in there touch my shit. You know I don't get down with that. After you retwist me up, I'ma head down to Joey's Barber Shop down on 18th and Vine or I might hit the homie Greg up to get a lineup."

"Well, let's go to the kitchen first to wash this shit and get you started after we wash this nappy shit."

We walked in the house and to the kitchen, she walked off to go grab all the stuff she needed to wash my shit. Baby girl got jokes today about my hair, but I will let her rock with that shit today only. She was telling the truth, my shit does look like that nigga Nappy dreads shit right now. She came back in sat everything on the counter and began to turn the water on to get it to the temperature of liking.

"Come on, Cuz. Lets get that shit washed, put your head under this water."

I bent my head down in the sink and that water running over my head felt so good right now. She massaged the shampoo into my head as she was massaging my head that shit started feeling good. She starting rinsing the shampoo out my hair then moved on to condition it after she was done she ringed the excess water out my hair then placed a towel over my head to dry my hair. Then headed back in so she can get started on retwisting. Three hours later, I was finally done. I tried to pay her, but she wouldn't take my money, saying it was on the house since I just got home. I was ok with that. I booked her for another appointment in two weeks. Then headed out the house to head to the crib.

Pulling up to the crib, I noticed Cortez still wasn't back, so before I even pulled into the driveway. I went towards Sarah's house. Soon as I pulled up, I saw his car was still sitting there, so I parked down the street then hopped out to go take a look. Creeping around the house, I heard loud moans. I didn't need to see or hear anymore, so I walked back to my car then sped towards the crib. Pulling in the driveway, I parked and headed inside. As I walked in, I smelled my favorite meal in the air: Spaghetti and Cheese Texas Toast.

I walked into the kitchen, and Tonia was dancing around the kitchen, setting shit on the table. I just stood there watching her dance. My baby had some moves on her. Just standing there watching her had my dick getting hard. As I was adjusting myself, she looked up at me after setting the last dish on the table. When she saw me adjust myself, she smiled and walked over to me. As soon as she got to where I was standing, she dropped down to her knees and unbuckled my pants. Pulling my dick out, she began to lick the head then deep throat my shit. I looked down at her, and what I saw almost made me nut right then and there. She was getting sloppy with it, spiting all over my dick and all over her mouth.

"Aww fuck, girl! If this is what I come home to everyday, I'mma make you my wife for damn sure. Fuck, ma."

She began to work harder at getting this nut. My dick hitting the back of her throat had me nutting in no time. I shot my seeds down her throat, and baby girl swallowed that shit then opened her mouth to show me. She licked her lips, rose to her feet and licked her lips then walked off towards the bathroom. I stuffed my pole back into my pants. Then went to wash my hands and wash my dick up.

I changed into some baller shorts then went back towards the kitchen to have dinner with, my bitch. When I got to the kitchen, I saw she was making mine and her plate. As I sat at the table, she set my plate in front of me along with a cup of tropical punch Kool-

Aid and sat next to me with her plate. We sat eating in silence, and this shit tasted amazing. Baby girl could throw down for damn sure. After finishing up with dinner, we cleared the table and I helped her load the dishes in the dishwasher. After we finished loading the dishes, I headed to my room to lay down for the night. Soon as my head hit the pillow, I was out.

Looking over at the clock, I noticed it was three in the morning, but all I heard was yelling throughout the house. Getting up out the bed, I walked out of the room. Looking to the left and then the right, I finally saw Cortez and Tonia arguing as they were walking towards the room, so I spoke up.

"What the fuck y'all doing up this late and arguing for?"

"Oh, I'm sorry, Cornell. I didn't mean to wake you, but your brother just got in and came home smelling like another bitch. He claims he is so faithful, but I believe otherwise seeing how he came in smelling like another bitch."

I just shook my head, "'Cuz, please tell me you ain't fucking another bitch when you got a woman who cooks and cleans for yo' ass?"

"'Cuz, I ain't discussing my relationship with yo' ass. Now get the fuck out my face with that shit. Tonia, come on to the room so we can talk."

"Nah, I'm good. I'm going to the guest room to lay down. Fuck you and that bitch you were with tonight."

She turned to go down the hall, went to the guest room and slammed the door. I turned to go back into my room, but my brother grabbed my arm and yanked me back around. I snatched away from him.

"'Cuz, what the fuck is you grabbing on me for?"

"Nigga, everything was cool 'til you brought your ass home from jail. What the fuck did you do to my girl to make her think I was fucking around on her?"

"I ain't did shit to your girl; you did. Shit, I see what she talking about. I smell that cheap as perfume on your ass. If I didn't know any better, I would say that it's Sarah's perfume but it can't because she left years ago, right?"

This nigga looked shocked that I put it together so damn fast, but I didn't give two fucks what he felt. He was gonna know that I knew what was going on with him. I smiled while this nigga looked shocked.

"Nigga, she has been gone. The fuck wrong with you? Plus, I wouldn't mess with shit that you done had anyway."

I smiled as he was talking, knowing what I know.

Chapter 5

Cortez

Standing here talking to this nigga as he grilled me about fucking Sarah, I had to get away from him before I tell him the real deal. I don't want him to find out that I been fucking Sarah this whole time and that we have a kid together. I've been fucking her since she was supposed to leave and I just got her a crib where he would least expect her to be. But she has been working with me for the last five years now to get back at his ass. She was the one who helped me get that cop on my team to take my brother down. The cop that also happens to be her brother. Now I just had to make sure that he didn't find out about either one of them.

Walking towards my room, I slammed my door and went to shower. Turning the shower on to the temperature of my liking, I washed my ass then got out. I dried off, went to my room, grabbed my briefs out the drawer and some basketball shorts, putting them on. I walked out my room back into the hallway where my brother was standing there knocking on the guest bedroom door, trying to get Tonia to answer. I knew she wasn't going to open it, so I just stood there and watched for a minute. Next thing I saw was her open the door to let him in. So I walked towards the door and I could hear them whispering about something. I knocked on the door to see if she would even open it and got no luck. So at this point, I started bamming on her door. Still got no answer.

"Open this fucking door right now, Tonia!"

"Fuck you, Cortez! I don't want to talk to you or see you, so leave me the hell alone."

"Bitch, I ain't going no fucking where 'til you open this damn door so you might as well open the door. It's funny that you let my brother in but not me."

"She only let me in so I can talk to her and get her to calm down. So shut the fuck up and let me talk to her with your crybaby ass. Yo' ass has always been a crybaby. Damn, let me help y'all get y'all shit together."

"Fuck both y'all bitches."

I turned to walk off to my room to get dressed. I wasn't about to stay here with both these bitches. It's bad enough that my brother is staying here, but now my fiancée is starting with her shit, thinking I'm cheating again. Granted, I am, but still, I had her thinking that I was being faithful. After I got dressed, I grabbed my phone and keys then headed out. Walking past the room Tonia was in, I could have sworn I heard kissing, but maybe I was just tripping.

Fuck that shit right now, I had to get the fuck up out of here before I kill my brother and Tonia. They were on some bullshit right now, and I ain't got time for that shit right now. Slamming the front door, I walked to my car, speeding off towards Sarah's crib. I arrived at her crib in no time. Jumping out my ride, I walked up to the door and used my key to unlock the door. I headed to Sarah's room, where she was laying there knocked out, where I left earlier from putting her ass to sleep after I sexed her real good. I walked back out to go check on my kid. Peeking in the room, I saw my young life knocked out, sucking on his thumb. We tried to get him not to, but that was an epic fail, so we just gave up. Shutting his door back, I walked back into the room I shared with Sarah when I'm here. I got undressed down to my briefs then climbed in bed, wrapping my arms around her.

"I thought you were going home to your wife. What happened?"

"Shit, she wanted to argue and shit, so I came back here. What, you don't want me here either?"

"I didn't say that, babe. I was just asking. Now go to sleep."

I guess she was done talking about it. So I just nuzzled my face into her neck and fell fast asleep.

The next morning...

I walked towards my son's room, looking in and there they were talking and getting dressed for his first day of kindergarten. I still couldn't believe my baby boy was going to school this year. I walked further in his room and they both looked up at me, smiling.

"Daddy, what you doing here? I thought you were going to be working today? You lie."

"Haha, son. Daddy wanted to be here for your first day of school. I couldn't miss that, son. Now come give yo' daddy some love."

He ran over to me and hugged me. As I hugged him, I just was thinking that I should be here with them every day instead of being with Tonia. I didn't love her anyway. I only got with her for the pussy just so I can brag that I bagged that bitch, but it went on far too long, and I ended up asking her to marry me on some drunken shit. I didn't want to marry her, that's why I wasn't even involved in her planning for this wedding. As far as I'm concerned, fuck that wedding and fuck her and my brother. They probably were fucking all night or something, but what did I care for when I had my own thing going on with Sarah. Releasing my son, I looked down at him looking all fly for his first day.

"Look at you, Cortez, you looking all fly for your first day of school. You gonna be fly like daddy, huh boy?"

"I sure am, Pops. I'm gonna be just like you when I grow up."

I laughed at my lil' man wanting to be like me. I just hoped and prayed he ain't gonna be the scheming type like me. After the shit I put my brother through, I don't want my son to be the same way. I want him to be better than me in all aspects of his life. I looked over at Sarah and she was smiling so big.

"What you smiling like that for, girl?"

"Babe, I'm just so happy right now. You being here for our son's first day of school means everything to me. But let me get him to the bus stop. I will be right back then I can cook you some breakfast and we can eat together if you want to, that is."

"That sounds great, ma. I will be here waiting. I'mma go jump in the shower while you take lil' man to the bus stop."

She grabbed his book bag and they headed out the door. I walked back into the room and looked in the closet to see if I had something here to wear sometimes I did bring clothes over here. I didn't see any of the clothes I left here, so I went out to the car to get the overnight bag that I have in the trunk for cases like these. Popping my trunk, I looked around and grabbed the bag and closed the trunk. As I looked around the neighborhood, I saw an unfamiliar car, but I didn't pay it any mind because nobody knew about Sarah and my son. At least to my knowledge, no one knew about them.

I walked towards the house and then looked back, that same car was now speeding down the street. I looked on to see if I could tell who it was, but the windows tinted. Now I was going to have to be on alert when I come out here to see my son and Sarah. I don't know who that could be, but I sure in the hell was going to find out. Closing the front door, I went back towards the room to get in the shower. Grabbing a towel and wash towel, got the temperature to my liking and washed my ass a good two times before I got out. Opening my bag, I grabbed my briefs and my blue **DBK (DopeBoy Kicks)** shirt and hoodie out and my blue true religion jeans. I got dressed, then headed out of the room to see Sarah was already back in the kitchen cooking. Walking into the kitchen, I grabbed her from behind and kissed her neck.

"You smell good, girl. You got me wanting to slide up in that good shit."

"Boy, move your ass and go sit down while I cook breakfast for us."

She pushed me off her, so I just turned and walked into the living room. I sat and watched the news until she told me breakfast was ready. There was so much shit going on in this world today and kids were dying every damn day. I know I run the streets, but I don't want any parts in these kids dying each day. My team knows that women and children are off-limits. I sat there for a little while 'til Sarah brought my plate to me. We both sat there and ate in silence while watching tv. We both must have been in deep thought. After I finished up my food, I got up, and Sarah stood up as well.

"Babe, I'm gonna get out of here. I got some business to take care of so I will see you later on. Ok?"

"Ok, babe."

I leaned down and hugged and kissed her lips. I grabbed my phone and keys then headed out to my car. Getting in, I sped off towards my house to see what was going on there, then I was going to head to the label. As I pulled up, I noticed that there weren't any cars in the driveway, but I pulled in any way to go check it out. Walking inside, I didn't hear any talking, so I walked around the house. As I walked around, I looked in my brother's room, and he wasn't there, so I walked down a little further into the room that Tonia was sleeping in. What I saw was a surprise to me. I never thought that I would be looking at my brother fucking my girl like I used to. I should have pulled out on them, shot both they asses, but at this point, I didn't give a fuck. I loved this girl just like I loved Sarah, but Tonia fucking my brother was a deal-breaker, and I was going to sit out here and wait on they ass to come out the room.

I walked to my room, went to my safe, grabbed my gun, and went back to the living room to wait on both their asses to come out. I waited for a good hour before they both decided to walk out of the room, fixing their clothes. I stood up and pointed my gun at both of them. As they got closer, they finally noticed me standing there with my gun on them.

"So, do you two bitches wanna tell me what the fuck I walked in on? And don't fucking lie to me, I saw Cornell fucking you."

"L—l—look, Cortez, I love you and all, but you haven't been making me happy for some years now, and me knowing that you are cheating with some bitch just pushed me further away. I didn't plan on falling for your brother, but I did. I'm not in love with you anymore; well I never was in love with you. I'm in love with Cornell."

"I love the fuck outta you, girl! Why the fuck would you do this to me and with my fucking brother at that? FUCK! And you, Cornell. Why would you sleep with my girl? The woman I'm supposed to be marrying?"

"Look nigga, I'm glad you found out. It's time that we sit down and talk anyway, so Tonia, have a seat and Cortez, put the fucking gun down now. We are gonna have a civilized conversation. No arguing and no fighting right now. Its time we have this conversation anyway."

Tonia had a seat, and he sat next to her. I tucked my gun away then took a seat on the opposite couch. I looked at both of them, and they looked at each other than my brother finally spoke up.

"Look, Cortez, I want you to know something that I have been thinking about for five years now. It's time that you know that I know you are the fucking reason why I went down that night. I want you also to know that I have blamed you for five years now for the death of Stacee. Although, I loved her. Shit, I still do, but I am in love with Tonia, and she is mine now. So you might as well just let her go, or we can go to war over that too. I do know that we will be going to war over you sending the police after me that night and for Stacee."

"Nigga, fuck you! You can't have her. I fucking love this girl; she is mine."

"Look, I followed you yesterday after you left here, saying you were going back to the label and to check on things with the street when yo' ass didn't do none of that shit, 'Cuz."

"Ok, sooo what does that mean?"

"It means that I know where you were yesterday and all last night, nigga."

"Wait. What the fuck you mean, you know where he was yesterday and last night?" Tonia asked.

Chapter 6

Tonia

Hearing that Cornell knew where the fuck Cortez was did something to me, so I got up and went back into the room I was sleeping in, slamming the door. I had to get the hell out of here right now. I went to the room I used to share with Cortez, grabbed my bag, and started packing some stuff up. After I packed a bag, I walked out of the room towards the living room. I could hear these two going back and forth still.

"Nigga, I don't give a damn what the fuck you think, you can't have my girl. I told your dumb ass I love her and that's final. We can shoot it out or fight it out, I gives no fucks, 'Cuz. Now you can pack yo' shit and get the fuck up out of my house. We don't need or want you here."

"But see, that's where you are wrong, Lil' Brother. See, yo' girl loves me and I love her. She needs and wants me here, so what you saying doesn't matter. You got yours coming though. Payback is a bitch. Trust and believe that."

I heard footsteps coming my way, so I hurried and ducked back in my room, locking the door.

Knock...knock...

"Who is it?"

"It's me, Cornell. Open the door, ma so we can talk. I know you feel some type of way about what was said out there."

"You're right, I do feel some type of way but I ain't in the mood to talk to you or him about it right now. I just want to be alone, so I can process everything please."

"Ma, that's not what we 'bout to do. You not shutting me out. Open this door, so we can talk or I will kick it down now."

Fuck it. I swung the door open and stood there waiting on him to talk. But he didn't say anything. He pushed right past me and sat down on the bed waiting on me to close the door. I closed the door, walked over to the dresser, and stood there so he can say what he got to say.

"Speak, nigga. I don't have all day. I have somewhere to be in a little while."

"You ain't even got nowhere to be 'til later when we go look at that shop you want to get so shut yo' mad ass up and listen. Ok, so yesterday when I left here, I followed my brother. He went to a chick house, yes, but after I saw a chick open the door, I sped back off. I didn't stay to see anything else. I went to handle my business. So you can't be mad at me right now, Ma. I wasn't tryna hurt you; I was just trying to get more info on what was going on. I didn't even want him to find out about us yet. Before I brought the info to you I wanted to have everything to give you. Baby, look, I love you, and I haven't felt this way about anyone, and I do mean anyone since Stacee. You know what I went through when I lost her, I can't lose you too."

"Look, I understand that, but you still should have told me what was going on or what you saw. You know I love you, but I can't stay in this house anymore."

"Then we can leave and find somewhere else to stay. We don't have to stay here if you don't want to. We can go to a hotel 'til we find a house. It's all up to you, bae."

"I was going to a hotel anyway, but I don't know if I wanna go with you. I need to be alone and think. You just told my fiancée that I love you when I wasn't even ready to tell him, then you knew he went to a chick house when he left here."

"I'm sorry for hurting you that way. I never meant to hurt you, please forgive me, babe. I know I should have talked to you first before I opened my mouth to Cortez about you loving me, but I let him get under my skin, and I shouldn't have. Like I told you, I love you, and I don't want to be without you, ma."

"Ok, look. I forgive you, but please don't let anything like this happen again. I can't take being lied to. I love yo 'ass too much to go through what I went through with your damn brother. Lord, I fell in love with brothers. How is that possible?"

"Man, look. Sometimes we can't help who we love. Our heart wants what it wants, and our hearts wanted each other; we can't control that love. Now let's pack up our stuff and get out of here while he is gone."

Cornell turned to walk out of the room, and I went to my room that I shared with Cortez to pack up the rest of my clothes and toiletries. After packing up everything I needed, I walked out the room carrying the bags that I could carry to the front room and setting them by the door for Cornell. I sat on the couch waiting on Cornell to come out the room with his stuff. As I was sitting there, I got lost in my thoughts. Thinking about where things went wrong with Cortez. I still couldn't understand what I did to him for him to switch up on me.

"Tonia, you ready to go, ma?"

"Yeah, let's get out of here."

We walked out of the house, but as soon as we walked out, Cortez was pulling up. Cornell just continued to bring our bags to the car with no care in the world that his brother was pulling up. I didn't even say anything. I just popped the trunk and then got in the car to start it up. As I sat there waiting on Cornell to finish loading the car, Cortez came over to my car and snatched my door open. Fuck, I should have locked that mothafucka. But I wasn't thinking. I just wanted to get out of here.

"Oh, so you think you 'bout to leave me for my brother? Bitch, you got me fucked up. Get your bitch ass out this fucking car."

"Nigga, I am leaving your ass, and I do love your brother. So you can have whatever bitch you been fucking with. I don't care anymore; the wedding is off."

I took my ring off and threw it at him. Cornell had finally put the last bag in the car, came around to my side, pushed Cortez out of the way, and shut my door back. After he shut my door, I locked it so he couldn't open my door back up. As I watched them go back and forth, I saw Cornell swing on Cortez, and they began to fight. Cornell was getting the best of Cortez. I didn't want to get out and stop them, just in case that distracted Cornell. So I just watched on. The next thing I saw was Cortez falling on the ground and Cornell standing over him yelling in his face. Cornell walked around to the other side of the car to get in. I put my seat belt on then drove off to the hotel we were going to be staying at. We both sat there in our thoughts. We were going to go to stay at the Hilton in Kansas City, Kansas.

"I'm sorry you had to fight your brother. You shouldn't have to fight your brother over me."

"Look, it was going to happen one way or another. He is the reason I was in jail in the first place, and the reason why Stacee and my child is dead, and I will never forgive him for that."

"But I still don't want y'all fighting over me though. I love you for even doing that, but I hate that I'm coming between the two of you."

"I understand that, baby, and I love you too, but don't think of you coming between us because we have been this way, way before you. He has always been jealous of me. Hint, why he took over the streets when I did that bid."

We pulled up to the hotel and I went inside to check in while Cornell grabbed our bags. As I was checking in, I thought about what he said. I didn't know that Cortez was behind any of that, that had gone down.

"Ma'am, Ma'am, I need your payment please."

"Oh, yeah. I'm sorry, sir. I just spaced off for a minute. Here you go."

I waited for him to hand me my bank card back. Feeling a presence behind me, I looked back and saw Cornell behind me with some of our bags.

"Ok, here is your room key. Thank you for staying at the Hilton Garden Inn."

"Thank you."

I grabbed my room key and we both walked towards the elevator, heading to the room. Getting on the elevator, I pushed the fifth floor. We both stood there lost in our thoughts. The elevator doors came open and we headed towards the room we would be staying in. I went to look around and I knew that I wouldn't be staying here longer than one night.

"Babe, we gonna have to find a new hotel tomorrow cause this sho' ain't gonna work."

"Girl, this room is fine. Quit tripping."

"I'm not tripping, bae. I don't like it."

"Fine, girl, whatever. Get online and find one that you will like then." I ran into his arms as soon as he set the bags down. I hugged him tight ass hell thanking him for agreeing with him. "Why you hugging me like that, girl?"

"Because I love you, boo. Now come and give me some of that daddy dick."

"You ain't gotta tell me twice. I've been waiting to climb up in that pussy anyway."

He pushed me back on the bed and stripped me out of my clothes. He kissed down my neck then made his way down to my breasts. He showed each one some attention then kissed down my body more, getting to my middle. He started kissing my inner thigh then making his way to my pussy. As he started kissing my middle lips, I got wet as fuck. He was licking my clit viciously.

"Oh, shit. I'm 'bout to cum."

"Let that shit go then, baby."

He didn't have to tell me twice. I let that shit go. He wiped his mouth then stripped out his clothes. Looking down at his long, thick pole, I was so amazed at how thick and sexy his dick was. Licking my lips, I sat up, crawling to the edge of the bed. He walked over towards the bed, standing in front of me. I looked up at him then I looked down at his pole. Taking him into my mouth, I began to suck his dick just like he liked it- sloppy. I was deepthroating him and as his dick hit the back of my throat, he rolled his eyes to the back of his head.

"Aww fuck, girl! Suck yo' dick just like that. Nice and sloppy just like that. If you keep sucking my dick like this, I'm going to make you my wife."

I kept sucking his long pole using my hands as I jacked his dick. He started pumping his dick into my mouth then released his seeds down my throat. Sitting up on the bed, I looked up into his eyes and smiled.

"Damn girl, you ain't playing no games tonight."

I shrugged my shoulders, smiling at him. He pulled me to the edge of the bed and then began to slowly ease the head of his dick inside my pussy. That shit felt amazing. As he was sliding in and out of my middle, I was releasing on his pole.

"Awww shit, girl! You cumming all over this dick."

"Mmhhh, yes, baby! Fuck yesss!"

He flipped me over then began to pound my kitty. I was feeling him in my stomach with each long, deep strokes. I felt his dick swell up and I knew he was cumming.

"Awww fuck, girl! I'm 'bout to cum. Cum with me, mama."

He didn't have to tell me twice I released all down his dick. Then I felt his semen coat my walls as he pumped in and out my middle.

"Argggg fuck girl."

He laid down next to me, trying to catch his breath. I trying to catch my breath as well.

Chapter 7

Cornell

After fucking my girl, I was ready to lay it down 'til it was time to go look at this location for Tonia's tattoo shop. I was happy that I could help her put her dreams into reality. My brother never wanted her to do any of that. I wanted to support my girl in everything that she wants to do. I'm a thug ass nigga, but I can be everything my girl wants and needs. Meaning I got a soft side, but I also have that mean side of me where I don't let a mothafucka get over on me.

Two hours later...

"Tonia mama, its time to get up so we can go look at these locations for your tattoo shop, Ma."

"Ughhh! Do we have to go right now? I just want to sleep a little longer, baby."

I pulled the covers off her body then she curled up in a ball still laying there, so I went to go grab a bucket of ice. When I came back to the room, she was still laying there in the bed, curled up in a ball. I walked over to the bed and dumped the bucket of ice on her.

"Arggghhh! Nigga, what the fuck you do that for?"

"So you will get your ass up and get ready, so we can go and look at these locations."

"Fine. I'm getting up, damn, but you didn't have to throw ice on me."

"I sure did 'cause yo' ass wouldn't get up when I tried to wake you up."

I walked out of the bedroom and went into the living area to sit and watch tv 'til she was ready to go. I was sitting there thinking that maybe I didn't have to hurt my brother. If he would turn everything back over to me, but I also have him as my right hand. I know that it may not work out that way because I could end up right back where I just was. And I don't want that shit at all. I will never go back to jail. It may be only one way this is going to work, but I know that will hurt my mother if she loses her other son. Just thinking about all that was going on and what the outcome could be if things go the way that I want them to go. I don't want to have to kill my brother, but if it comes down to it, then I will do what I have to do.

One hour later...

We were now walking around the first location. It was nice, but I don't know if this was the spot that she should choose, but it was her choice.

"So what do you think of this location? If you don't like it, we have a few more we could go look at, if you would like?" The realtor asked.

"Well, I like it, but it just doesn't speak to me. Yeah, I would like to see what the others look like before I make my final decision," Tonia replied.

The realtor nodded her head, agreeing with Tonia. So we all headed out the building to our cars. I followed behind the realtor to the next location. As we were pulling up to the next location, I looked at it and was in awe. But again, it wasn't my choice; it was Tonia's choice. This was her Tattoo shop, not mine. We both got out of the car, following behind the realtor. As we walked inside the building, I looked around, and this spot was perfect. Looking over at Tonia, I knew she was in love with this one.

"Tonia, what you think, Ma? Is this the spot for you? 'Cause if not, I'm taking this for myself. This spot is dope," I stated.

"Babe, I love this one. It is what I've been looking for. I think this is it, but I still think I should look at the others to make sure. But I don't know I do love this one."

"Ms. Keys, we can look at the others if you would like. My schedule is freed up all day, just in case the first few weren't what you were hoping for. It's your choice," The realtor replied.

Tonia stood there thinking for a minute before she finally looked over at me then stated that this was the one she was going to go for. I was super excited for my girl. Her dream was finally coming true to open her tattoo shop. I was happy that I could help her. With the little bit of money I had stashed away, I was going to help her get this shop if she needed it.

"So, let's discuss the price of this building. Let's head back to the office and handle everything there," the realtor stated.

"Let's get it done then," I replied.

Looking around the building, I knew she was gonna take over the world just like Ceasar did from Black Ink Crew. Yea, I knew all about that nigga name Ceasar. He was a boss a nigga from what I saw on tv while I was locked up. He was making moves out in this fucked up world. He had plenty of enemies, but he still didn't let that stop him. It meant a lot seeing a successful black man doing big things like he was doing. I wanted the same thing for Tonia.

We all headed to the realtor's office. As we were driving down 71 highway, I was looking around to make sure nothing out of the ordinary was happening. When I was looking in the rearview mirror, I saw a car following behind me. That got my attention real quick.

"Babe, call the realtor and tell her we will be right behind her. We have to make a pit stop right quick. And hand me that gun out the glove box."

"Is everything ok?"

"Don't worry, babe. Just do what I asked to please."

She didn't ask any more questions and did what I asked of her. I got off on the next exit. Making a left turn, I saw that the car was still following us, so I made a right turn. And again, the car made the same right turn. So I pulled over to the next gas station I came to and hopped out. As I hopped out, the person in the car rolled down their window and started shooting. I yelled for Tonia to get down. I closed the door to the car, got down then started bussing my gun at whoever was bussing their guns at me. As I looked on to see who it was, I got hit up in the chest then fell back. But seeing that the shooter was my brother broke my heart because I thought that it wouldn't come to this, but I guess I thought wrong.

Falling to the ground, I heard tires screech off. Then I faintly heard Tonia yelling my name out, but I couldn't answer her as I was fading in and out. I was slowly fading away. I never thought that my life would end this way. I just found the love of my life and was going to do right by her, just like I would have done for Stacee if she was still here.

I was trying to fight through and stay here, but it was starting to get harder and harder to keep my eyes open. This must have been what Stacee was feeling the night that she was taken from me. But I didn't wanna go and be with her just yet I still had a lot more life to live. I wanted to show Tonia the world and make her my wife. If I should survive this, I was going to make her my wife. No matter how my brother feels.

Chapter 8

Tonia

Watching Cornell take shallow breaths trying to stay with me was hard as fuck. I didn't know if he was going to make it or not. Looking around, I saw people with their phones out recording and taking pictures; some were even on their phones calling for an ambulance. I was kneeled next to him, trying to get him to keep his eyes on me but also trying to see who would have done this to him. Who would want to take him from me like this? Then it dawned on me that the only person I know about that would want him dead is his brother. This was going to hurt Ms. Bishop if she loses Cornell like this.

Looking down at Cornell's eyes, I noticed they were closed, and his chest wasn't rising and falling. I knew that he was gone, but I tried anyway to get him to open his eyes, but he wouldn't. I didn't know what to do, but then I heard sirens. I was happy to see that they were finally coming to help my man because I sure as hell don't know what to do.

The police arrived first on the scene. One officer walked over to me and tried to pull me away from Cornell, but I wasn't moving until the paramedics came and helped him. Finally, the fire truck pulled up along with an ambulance. They hopped out, moving quickly to get him on the stretcher and in the truck. I got in the car but before I could pull off one of the officers stopped me from leaving.

Ma'am, you can't leave yet. We have questions to ask you first."

"I can give two fucks about your questions right now. My man needs me. If you have questions for me, meet me at the hospital. Didn't you see the same thing I saw? When my man was placed in that ambulance, he wasn't even breathing."

"You can either answer our questions here or we take your disrespectful mouth ass downtown and book you and then question you down there," the officer contorted.

I huffed out a breath and turned the car off, but before getting out the car, I made sure to call Cornell's mother to let her know that she needed to get to the hospital because Cornell was just shot. After hanging up with her, I got out the car then leaned up against it, waiting on the officer to start with his questions.

"Ok, so Miss...?"

"It's Tonia Keys."

"Tonia, can you tell me what happened here today?"

"We were headed back to the realtor's office to go discuss some prices of a building that I was looking at to open my tattoo shop, when my man Cornell Bishop noticed that we were being followed, I guess. We pulled up to the gas station, and he hopped out the car to see what was up. And next thing I know, shots rang out, and Cornell was laying on the ground with a gunshot wound to the chest. The car skirted off, and I hopped out the car running to him. I had to help him somehow, but I didn't know what to do."

"Did you get a good look at who was in the car that shot at your boyfriend?"

I looked up at the officer then down the street and noticed that the same car that shot at us was now sitting down on the corner watching on as I talked to the officer. I wasn't gonna let Cortez scare me. No matter if it wasn't right to snitch, I was going to get justice for my man if he didn't make it through this battle he was bout to be fighting.

"Ms. Keys, I'ma ask you once again. Did you see who the person was in the car that was shooting at your boyfriend?"

"Yes, I did see who it was."

"Ok, tell me who it was then."

"It was his brother, my ex, Cortez Bishop."

The officer looked at me, shocked at what I just said, but I didn't care. He can judge me if he wanted to, but I'm not ashamed that I had been messing with two brothers. I loved Cortez at one point in time, but he wasn't the man for me, and he couldn't keep his dick in his pants.

"Don't judge me. It is what it is. I'm not ashamed of what has transpired between the three of us. Only thing that I am ashamed of is Cornell being shot over me and him being in love."

"No judgment here, ma'am. I was just shocked that you said it was his brother that shot him. Do you know where we can find Mr. Bishop right now?

I looked up to see if he was still in the same spot, and he was just like a dummy. I nodded my head, then looked over at the officer and told him that he was in his car on the corner down there, watching everything that was going on right now. The officer looked down the street after I stated where he was, Cortez sped off. Fuck, I knew he was going to run and hide now. The officer radioed for other officers to go after Cortez. He even gave them a plate number, which I didn't know he had gotten off the car from where we were standing, but I guess he had good enough eyes to see that far away.

"Can I go now? I have answered all of your questions and I need to get to the hospital?"

"Sure, go ahead. If I need anything else, I will be in contact with you. Please give me your number to contact you."

I recited off my number, then got in the car and sped my ass to the hospital. Pulling up at Research medical center, I parked and headed inside to see what was going on. As I walked inside, I saw Mama Bishop sitting there with tears in her eyes. Right then and there, I knew that my man had to be gone. This just couldn't be life. I was just getting started with him. I let the tears fall as I walked over to Mama Bishop so she could tell me what I already knew was my faith.

"Mama Bishop, what are they saying?"

"Right now, honey, they are trying to revive him before they take him to surgery. He wasn't responsive when he arrived here. So they have to revive him before they can take him right on back to surgery. The bullet missed his heart from what they could tell me right now. They are gonna do everything that they can to remove the bullet and revive him."

"Oh my God, this is all my fault?"

"Chile, what you mean this is all your fault? How is this your fault?"

"It's no easy way to say this, but I have been seeing Cornell for the last three years now since your other son has been seeing someone else. I didn't mean for any of this to happen, but I just fell in love with Cornell over the years. Cortez found out and they had big ass fight at the house. Long story short, I broke up with Cortez, and now I'm with Cornell."

"Baby, I been knew about you and Cornell. He told me when you guys first started."

I looked over at her in shock that she even knew about us. I didn't even know he had told his mother anything about us. I hope that he will make it out of this alive.

"Mama Bishop, I'm sorry for everything that just happened."

"Listen, honey, you can't help who you fall for, but sometimes things happen that are beyond our control. The heart wants what the heart wants. There is no denying the heart for who it is meant to be with. Yes, it was wrong for y'all both to be messing with each other behind Cortez's back, but you didn't do anything wrong here. Cortez has always been jealous of Cornell. Cornell would always get more attention from his father, but I guess I am to blame. Cortez has a different father than Cornell. How that happen is another story for another day. But if I didn't step out on Cornell's father, then this wouldn't be happening."

"Wait, they don't have the same daddy? I thought they did. But they look just alike in every way."

"Yes, they do, but that's my genes that they picked up on."

I nodded my head as she spoke so freely about everything. I didn't even have to tell her who shot her son; she already knew it was Cortez that had did this. When we looked up, there was a doctor headed our way. We both stood up and waited for the doctor to call for Cornell's family.

"Family of Cornell Bishop?"

We walked over to him and then listened on as he spoke about what had happened during the surgery. Cornell coded on the table a few times, but each time they were able to revive him. They were also able to remove the bullet, but he was now in a medically induced coma to help him heal properly. I was happy that he was still here with us, but I was sad that he was in a coma. I just hope and pray that he wakes up soon.

I looked down at my phone that was ringing. I stepped away from Mama Bishop and the doctor as they were still talking.

"Hello, Ms. Keys. Are you guys still coming down to the office?'

"Ummm, we had a bit of an emergency. Can I come in tomorrow please?"

"Ok, sure. I will take it off the market and hold it for you until you can come in. I understand that things can happen so take your time and handle what you need to handle. I will not sell to anyone else."

"Oh my god, thank you so much. I will see you tomorrow for sure though. I can't lose this building; it's my dream."

We said our goodbyes and then hung up. I walked back over to Mama Bishop and the doctor as they were just now getting ready to take us to his room. I followed behind them lost in my thoughts on everything that had transpired over the last two years. We walked into the room that they had Cornell set up in. It seemed all so real to me. My baby was hooked up to all kinds of wires and monitors. Just looking at him like this brought tears to my eyes. Holding my body tight, I just let the tears flow freely. I looked at my man lying in that bed looking like he was on his death bed, but he wasn't these machines was breathing for him. Walking closer, I sat in the chair that was next to his bed and grabbed his hand to hold it, so he will know that I was here with him.

Chapter 9
Cortez

After I sped off from that gas station and saw the officer look my way, I knew that Tonia had told them that I was the one that shot my brother. I wasn't tryna shoot him. I was just trying to scare him. I didn't expect him to get out and shoot back at me, but he did, so I had to take him down. It was either him or me. I was headed to Sarah's house to go hideout. Tonia didn't know where she lived, so that was a blessing in disguise if I do say so myself. The only person that knew where she stayed was not talking anytime soon. I knew this would hurt my mother and father, but shit, that's on them. They didn't think I knew the real reason why my father showed Cornell more attention than he did me, but I did. I heard my parents arguing so many years ago about my paternity, and how he was treating me differently than he did

Cornell, and she just kept apologizing for the shit. That it was started my dislike for Cornell.

I pulled my car in the garage then got out and walked into the house to my son and Sarah on the floor playing. I was happy to see that they were enjoying life. Because mine would soon enough be over if the cops found out where I was laying low at. I hope they didn't come here to find me though. I know that this would break my woman's heart that she would maybe soon become a single mother. I walked over to the couch and took a seat then just watched on as I got lost in my thoughts. Looking up, I saw flashing lights coming from outside, so I got up to head to the window, and there they were right outside of the house.

"Sarah, baby, I'm sorry, Ma, but I'm 'bout to go away for a little while. I did something stupid, and I won't be around to help you raise our son."

"What the fuck you mean, you won't be around to raise our son? What the fuck did you do, Cortez?"

"Umm, I shot my brother. I think I killed him, and the cops are right outside your house."

"What the fuck you mean you shot and may have killed your brother?"

"JUST WHAT THE FUCK I SAID! I SHOT HIS ASS AND THINK I KILLED HIM. DON'T START THAT QUESTIONING SHIT! RIGHT NOW I DON'T HAVE FUCKING TIME TO EXPLAIN THIS SHIT TO YOU! RIGHT NOW THE COPS IS RIGHT OUTSIDE THIS FUCKING HOUSE! I HAVE TO GET THE FUCK OUTTA HERE, MA!"

"Don't be yelling at me, Cortez. I just asked a simple ass question. If you did it, you don't need to run. What type of man are you to shoot someone and then run? And not only that, the person you shoot is your fucking brother. That shit just ain't right. You need to take your ass out there and turn yourself in. I didn't sign up for this shit when we started fucking around with each other. Now you need to go."

I just shook my head, but I sat there thinking about what she just said. I know I was wrong for shooting my brother, but he shouldn't have shot back at my ass. I was just trying to scare him, not kill him or hurt him. I guess what Sarah was saying was true; I should turn myself in. I need to show my son that you have to be a man and take responsibility for your actions, and I was going to do just that. I got up off the couch and walked over to where Sarah and my son were and kissed them both, saying goodbye. I probably won't see them for a while.

As I walked out the house, there were guns drawn and cops standing behind their cars. I guess just in case I started shooting, they were taking cover. But I wasn't on that shit. I ain't ready to die, and I didn't want to be gone for life for killing cops. Shit, I'm already gonna be gone long enough away from my damn son. Holding my hands up, I walked out towards the officers. One of the officers walked towards me, telling me to turn around and get on the ground with my hands behind my back. I did just what he had asked me to do. The officer went on about reading me my rights then handcuffing me. I looked up into the house, and I saw my son standing there, looking on as I was getting handcuffed. I didn't want my son to see this shit at all. I was planning to walk towards the street, but these damn officers didn't let me get that far. FUCK!

The officer pulled me up off the ground, then walked me to the patty wagon. They helped me get in and shut the door. I was headed downtown to the county jail, fuck my life. I didn't need to be in there. That is not the place for me, but it is what it is. I gotta pay for my crimes. Just like Sarah said, I have to take responsibility for my actions. Sitting there lost in my thoughts, I didn't even notice that we came to a stop until the door to the van came open and another officer was pulling me out and dragging me into the jail. These mothafuckas was manhandling me like I was resisting or something when I did exactly what was asked of me. They think cause they have that damn badge that they could get away with whatever they wanted to do to us. But they got another thing coming this way.

"Come on, dawg, you ain't gotta manhandle me like that. I have followed all y'all damn rules, you ain't gotta treat me like this."

"Shut your stupid ass up and keep walking."

I just shook my head and walked on. Ain't no point in arguing with these punk-ass cops. I was just gonna keep quiet for now. Getting on the elevator, they took me to a holding cell until they were ready to process me in their system or whatever they need to do. I took a seat on one of the benches and looked around to see my surroundings. I can't just not know who was around me. What type of nigga would I be if I'm just sitting here and not knowing who was sitting around me? It could be an enemy or anything. I ain't got time for that shit. I didn't see any enemies or anything, so I just sat there and waited for them to call my name.

Two hours later...

An officer finally came to get me so I could get processed in. This shit took too damn long and I still haven't even got my phone call yet. I guess they do shit on their own time. I got fingerprinted, and they took my photo then gave me a jail jumpsuit to put on. I had to stripe all the way butt ass naked. They had me bend over and cough. I don't know what that shit was for, but I did as they asked. I also felt violated in here with these men butt ass naked bending over. I ain't on no gay shit, so if they were on that shit, they might as well save that shit 'cause I don't get down like that.

I was finally able to put my jumpsuit they gave me on, and then they took me to an integration room where two detectives were sitting there waiting on me. They handcuffed me to the table then walked out of the room. I looked up at them and just shook my head. They think I'm going to talk to them without my lawyer.

"I don't have shit to say to y'all without my lawyer, so get me my phone call."

"You one real cocky son of a bitch, I see. You are going down for the attempted murder on your brother Cornell Bishop," one of the detectives replied.

I shrugged my shoulders and just sat there quiet as a church mouse. Like I said, I'm not talking to them without my lawyer present. Ain't nobody stupid, they think they can get you to talk without your lawyer so they can hold that against you in court. Well, I think the fuck not. We sat there for another twenty minutes before they finally got the hint that I wasn't talking.

One of them uncuffed me from the table and walked me out to a phone where I was later able to call my lawyer. Mr. Alverez has been the family lawyer for some time now. I hope he doesn't deny my case because of my brother, but shit, he getting paid, so his ass better take this fucking money.

"This is Alverez. How can I help you?"

"Alverez, it's Cortez Bishop. I need you downtown now. I'm in jail on attempted murder charges."

"I'm on my way, Mr. Bishop."

We disconnected the call then I was escorted back to my cell 'til my lawyer gets here. I must have been sitting in this cell before my lawyer finally got there. I was escorted back to the integration room where the officers and my lawyer was waiting on me and handcuffed to the table next to my lawyer.

"Ok, so let's start this over now that your lawyer is here, shall we."

"Detectives, first of all, I will need a minute alone with my client while we discuss his options and his case."

"Fine. We will give you about ten to twenty minutes alone, but that is it. We don't have all day to deal with this shit with your client."

They both got up and walked out the door. I turned to my lawyer then began to talk to him about everything that transpired today.

"OK, Cortez, tell me what the fuck is going on, so I know what I'm getting into with this shit."

"I shot Cornell. I wasn't trying to hurt him, but he shot back at me when I shot at him. I was only trying to scare him."

"Got dammit, Cortez, what the fuck was you thinking? I told your ass to leave it the fuck alone. Now I have to clean your shit up once again. I'm getting tired of cleaning up your damn messes, son."

"Pops, I know, man. I know. It's just hard knowing that he has my girl now, and he has always got all of his dad's attention, and he has always been the favorite son. Shit, I didn't even know you were my real father 'til one day I heard them arguing about the shit."

Yep, my lawyer is my biological father, but Cornell doesn't know that shit, and my parents don't know that I know this shit. When I found out who my father was, I went searching for him.

"Look, son, I will see what I can do to get you off this shit, but you have to stop this jealousy shit between you and your brother. You hear me?"

"Yeah, I got you, Pop. Just please get me out of here. I can't be locked down like this, I got a son to take care of."

"Well, I'm gonna do everything I can, son. Just sit there and don't say a word, you hear me?"

I nodded my head, and then five minutes later, those same two detectives came back in the room and took a seat across from us.

"So Mr. Bishop, are you ready to talk now?"

"Detectives, my client has admitted to me that he did, in fact shoot at his brother, but he wasn't trying to hurt him. He was in a state of shock from seeing his brother with his fiancée. What we are willing to do, since this is my client's first offense ever, is plead guilty but with a light sentence. Like I stated before, this is his first offense."

"You think you can get a lighter sentence for attempted murder because this is your first fucking offense? I think the fuck not. We are going to throw the book at your ass. What if you would have killed your brother, man? Come on, think about how that would look."

"I was just trying to scare him, I wasn't even trying to shoot him, man. Come on now, he is fucking my fiancée behind my fucking back, and I got mad and reacted. I won't do no shit like this again. I can't go down for this. I have a son to raise."

"Well, you should have thought about that before you decided to shoot at your brother."

They both got up and walked out of the room, leaving me and my lawyer to discuss what we could do next. I got to thinking about what we could do to get me out of here so I wouldn't be gone away from my son to damn long, but I couldn't come up with shit. I looked over at my pops, and then he looked up at me with this weird look on his face.

"You know I can try and get you moved from here to the medical facility to get you evaluated for mental illness. That would look good for your cases, son. I know you don't want to do that, but it may help you get out of this shit."

"Do what you got to do. I need to get out of here. Look, hit up my Sarah for me. She is my son's mother. Tell her I'm sorry that our son had to see that shit and that I'm doing everything I can to get home to them. I'm just going to let Cornell have Tonia. I haven't been in love with her for some time now. So it's best that we just cut our losses."

"I will handle everything, son. I may not have been there for you when you were growing up, but I'm here now. I'm going to do my very best to get you home to your son. I got you."

He stood up and walked out the room. Then after he walked out, another officer came in to escort me back to my cell. I laid down on the bench and just relaxed for a while until I knew if I was getting out or not. I just still couldn't believe I almost killed my brother. I was going to do everything I could to make it up to him. I had to make things right with him. Closing my eyes, I let sleep take over my body.

Chapter 10

Cornell

I didn't know what was going on. The last thing I remember was seeing my brother shoot at me when I hopped out my car. I know he shot me, but damn I know I ain't dead. I felt someone touching my hand, and from the scent that I smelled in the room,

I knew it was my baby, Tonia. She must have been by my side all this time I just couldn't open my eyes yet. I don't know why I couldn't wake up. I was trying my best to open my eyes, but just couldn't. I needed to let my baby know I was still alive. I wasn't leaving my baby in this world alone without me. Falling back into a deep sleep, I just relaxed my body and rested up.

Looking around, I didn't know where I was at, but I looked over and saw Stacee sitting on a bench, so I

walked over and sat next to her. I hugged her tightly, not wanting to let her go. I missed her so damn much.

"Cornell, baby, I want you to know that I don't blame you for what happened that day. It's ok to move on. I know you are seeing your brother's fiancée and that you did it behind his back. You shouldn't have done it that way, but look, that's not why I'm here. I'm here because you have to wake up and live your life, leave that street shit alone and open up that business you always said you wanted to open up. You just did a five-year bid. Now it's time to change your life around. You have a new girl now that loves everything about you. It's time to let that life go and do what's best for her. She is the one you should be marrying, you hear me? Let that stuff with Cortez go. He feels bad for what he did to you. Y'all need to bury the hatchet."

"But I don't even have all the money to start up that business. Stacee, things have been rough, but I'm gonna try and forgive him. But damn, Ma, he tried to kill me. He is the reason you're not here with me

anymore. It's all his fault for this shit. I hate having to live life without you."

"I know you do, but I'm fine. This is what God has planned for me. I am just happy that we spent as much time together that we were able to. You have to let that hurt go, so you don't hurt that girl Tonia. She needs you right now, and you and mama Bishop is all she has right now. Get it together, I mean it."

"Ok, ok, I will. I love you and miss you."

"I love you and miss you too."

I put my head down and just sat there lost in my thoughts for a minute longer. Stacee was right; it is time for me to leave this street shit alone 'cause look at me. I've been shot up, been in jail and lost my fiancée in these last five years. Now forgiving my brother, that was going to be a hard thing because he could have killed me. But I was going to try my hardest to forgive him the best way that I could. It was just going to take some time. No telling how much time it would take to forgive him.

Finally able to open my eyes, I looked around and didn't see my girl next to me, but when I looked to the right of me, she was laying on a little couch or whatever they call those things that pull out like a bed, sleeping soundly. I reached over for my call light to call a nurse or doctor.

"How can I help you?"

I couldn't talk because of the discomfort of something in my throat, so I just laid back to wait on the nurse or doctor to walk in. I laid there waiting for five more minutes before someone came walking in. I was surprised that Tonia hadn't woke up, even with that loud ass nurse over the call light shit. She was sleeping so soundly.

"Oh, you finally woke. I know your loved ones will be so happy. They have been here around the clock sitting with you over this last month that you have been in a coma, honey."

I looked at her as she talked about me. I couldn't believe that I had been in a coma this damn long. The nurse told me she would be right back with the doctor to get this damn tube out of my throat. I hope they hurry up and get this shit out of my throat soon cause this shit is not comfortable at all. Then I couldn't talk either I wanted to let my girl know that I was ok and that I was woke. The nurse did just what she said she was going to do and come right back in with the doctor. The doctor removed the tube, and then the nurse handed me a cup of water. I downed that cup and was ready for another. She refilled my cup, and then I downed that one as well.

"So, the nurse here says I have been in a coma for a month. Is that correct?"

"Yes, sir, it has been a little over a month. Mr. Bishop, you suffered a gunshot to the chest that actually missed your heart by a mere inch. You are lucky to be alive right now. We were not responsive when you were brought in, and you had coded on the table a few times during surgery. After the surgery, we placed you in a medically induced coma to give your body time to heal. We have been waiting on you to wake up about two to three weeks now," the doctor replied.

"Thank you, doc. I do appreciate all that y'all have done for me since I have been out for the count." I turned towards where Tonia was still sleeping and just shook my head. The nurse was checking my vitals, so while she was doing that, I was going to wake this girl the hell up somehow. Since I couldn't get out of this bed, I would have to yell at her to wake up. "Tonia Keys, wake your ass up, girl."

She jumped up out of her sleep after I called her name a few times. She looked around for a few minutes, then her eyes set in on me. She smiled and started crying, seeing that I was finally woke. She hopped up off the bed and ran over to where I was. She was crying and everything. I reached over to her and wiped her tears from her eyes.

"Baby, how long have you been woke?"

"Before he answers that, let me say this, then I will give you two some alone time." She nodded her head, then the doctor continued. "So, as we took your vitals, it looks like everything is fine, but you still have to take it easy. Now we will be getting out of here. Call me if you need me."

The nurse and doctor turned and left the room. We were finally alone in the room. I looked up at her and she was still crying like I was leaving her to fend for herself.

"Girl, stop all that crying; I ain't gone nowhere. I'm still here and I ain't going anywhere for a long time now, you hear me?"

"Yeah, I hear you. I'm just so happy that you are woke finally. Me and Mama Bishop, along with Papa Bishop, has been here every day checking on you."

"What about Cortez? Where is he?"

"He is in a mental hospital getting evaluated. Something about mental issues never being treated, and that's what caused him to shoot you."

"Bullshit, that nigga ain't got no mental issues. That's just a lie so he can get out of what he did to me. But look, I ain't 'bout to let that shit hold me back. If he gets out, he gets out. I have to forgive him cause we brothers, but I can't fuck with him like that right now 'til I'm ready."

"Well, let me call mama Bishop and let her know you are awake. She can explain this thing with your brother more. I will be right back."

She leaned down and kissed me on the cheek. I ain't want her to kiss my lips anyway since I ain't been able to handle my hygiene and brush my teeth yet. I laid back as I watched her walk out of the room. Her ass was starting to get thicker. If I didn't know any better, I would think my bitch was pregnant, but I believe she said she was on the pill or some shit. I would just have to ask her when she comes back into the room. I closed my eyes and just relished in the moment of still being here to change my life around. She doesn't know it yet, but I wasn't going back to the streets. I was going to turn everything over to my niggas, Red and Preston. They deserve it for holding shit down when I was away, making sure my brother doesn't run this shit in the ground. Them niggas were solid, no doubt.

A few minutes later, as I was dozing off, there was a knock at the door, then I heard some footsteps walking in. I peeked out the corner of my eyes and saw Sarah standing there with who I assume is my nephew. I closed my eye back quickly, hoping she didn't see me peeking at her, but I guess I was wrong.

"I know you are awake. I saw you peeking at me so gone and open them eyes back."

"Man, what the fuck do you want with yo' snake ass?"

"I came here on your brother's behalf. He asked me to come check on you since he couldn't do it his self. He feels bad for what he did to you."

"Well shit, he should feel bad. I lost a month of my life laying in this damn bed because he was on some jealousy shit. The fuck."

"I understand all that, but I just came by to do what he asked me to do. I will head out now."

As she was getting ready to walk out the door, in came Tonia. She looked at me then looked at Sarah but didn't say shit. She walked over to me and kissed my cheek, then sat back in the chair. Before Sarah could walk out of the room, Tonia stopped her.

"Sarah, it is right?"

"Yes, that is me."

"Don't leave just yet. You need to have a seat, and let's talk. Plus, I believe your son's father's family would like to meet your son since everyone is on the way here. And they didn't even know about this cute little boy since you and yo' nigga been hiding him from everybody."

"It wasn't even like that. I've wanted to tell you and the rest of the family about things for a year and a half, but he wouldn't let me say anything. I was tired of being a secret; my son shouldn't be anyone's little secret."

"You are right about that. Now come take a seat over here so we all can talk," Tonia replied.

Sarah took a seat in the chair by the window. It was quiet for a minute before the door opened and in walked my parents. See, I told y'all about how my father had left my mother when we were born, but I guess she and him got back together when I was locked up, which I didn't find out about 'til I got out and seen it for myself. I was mad at first, but I couldn't hold how I felt against him any longer. He is still my father; he will just have to explain why he walked out on us all those years ago.

"Baby, I'm so glad you are awake. God is so good," my mother confessed. She looked over by the window then noticed Sarah and her son sitting there. "Who are you?"

"I'm Sarah, I am Cortez's baby's mother. I've been seeing him for the last five years."

"What the fuck you mean, you been seeing my son for the last five years and you have a baby with him? Did you know he was engaged to this lady right here?"

"I knew they were seeing each other, but I didn't know they were engaged. If I would have known that, I would have never been still seeing him at all."

"Well, we were engaged but are no longer. I am no longer with him so you can have him, honey," Tonia sassed.

"Tonia, shut yo' stupid ass up 'cause you were in the wrong too for sleeping with his damn brother. Don't be throwing stones when you live in a glass house, heffa," Mama sassed back.

I laughed and continued to listen on to their conversation. After all that was going on, they were all sitting here getting along, but now it was my time to interrupt them because I needed to know what the fuck was going on with this nigga Cortez. Why did he hate me so much?

"I know y'all are all on your kumbaya bullshit, but can someone please tell me why the fuck my little brother hates me so fucking much to try and kill me? And don't y'all say some bull ass shit like 'cuz I was fucking his fiancée because clearly, he was fucking my jump off and lord knows how many other bitches. I know you two know what it is because Tonia said you would have to explain it all to me."

"Son, look. I'm not Cortez's biological father. That is the real reason why I left when I did all those years ago. I'm sorry that this is taking a toll on you and his relationship. I should have been man enough to stay and take care of the both of you, but at that time I couldn't wrap my head around your mother stepping out on me. Now I believe that plays a role in why he tried to kill you. Then also the fact that you ARE indeed sleeping with his ex-fiancée."

I shook my head and got pissed off at what the fuck my pops just told me. I couldn't believe I never knew my mother stepped out on my pops, but that does put things into perspective for me. So all this shit that had been going on has been building up and building up 'til he couldn't take it anymore, then he just snapped. I do believe he has some mental issues now that I think about it.

"So, do y'all think that he really has mental issues then?"

"Son, your brother was diagnosed with a very serious case of bipolar disorder when you guys were younger, but as he got older, he stopped taking his meds. There was nothing I could do about that after he moved out of the house. I use to sneak his pills in his food when he was a teenager, but I couldn't do the same thing I use to do because he moved out and stopped coming around so much once you got locked up," My mother replied.

"Wow, Mom, really? Why didn't you ever say anything? You been keeping a lot of fucking secrets. All this shit could have been avoided if you would have just said something. It took me getting shot for you to speak the fuck up, what type of shit is you on?"

"Now, hol' up, son. You are not going to talk to your mother like that. She is still your mother. She is not to blame here. We can't sit around here and point fingers at one another when the real person to blame is your brother."

My dad was right, but still, she should have told me that he was that fucking ill and needed to be on meds to survive out here.

"Look ma, I'm sorry. It just is a lot of shit to take in. I shouldn't have talked to you like that."

"You damn right, you shouldn't have, but look Sarah, baby, you can come by and bring our grandson around the house anytime. We will welcome him with open arms. You hear me, girl? Now let's all get out of here and let Tonia and Cornell get some alone time."

I don't know what the hell my mother was up to, but me and Tonia didn't need any alone time 'til I could get the fuck up out of this hospital. Then I can beat that pussy up like I wanted to. Shit, looking at how fat that ass is got my dick bricking up right the fuck now. I don't know if I can wait 'til I get home. She may have to just hop on this dick and ride that wave like it's 1999. Everyone else got up and walked out of the room, but before they left, they all said their goodbyes. I was kinda glad that they all were gone 'cause now that they left, I can talk to Tonia about what I wanted to talk to her about.

"Why are you staring at me like that, Cornell?"

"Shit, that ass looking fatter, and I missed that pretty ass face of yours. Damn, ma, you got me bricking up just looking at all that ass."

Chapter 11

Tonia

This nigga Cornell is a damn fool, talking about how fat my ass is. That nigga wanted some pussy, but he just woke up from being in a coma for over a damn month now. I didn't want him to regress and maybe even slip back into a coma.

"Boy, shut yo' stupid ass up. You ain't getting no pussy; you just woke up from a coma."

"So fucking what? You can still hop on this dick and ride this wave like it's muthafucking 1999. Now lock that door and come ride this muthafucking dick. Quit acting like yo' pussy ain't wet right now thinking about cumming all over this dick. Like yo' pussy ain't throbbing right now thinking about slow grinding that phat ass pussy on this dick. Quit acting like that and come on, girl. We ain't got all damn day before these doctors come back into this room."

"Look Cornell, if I do this for you. Not saying that I will, but it's a **BIG IF** I do this, nigga, you better let me take it easy and not that rough shit you are used to. You did just wake up, nigga, from being shot in the chest."

"Ok. Ok, ma, fine. Do what you need to do. It's your world anyway."

I smiled at him, got up back out of my seat and went and locked the door. Stripping out of my clothes slowly, I walked over towards the bed and pulled the cover down towards his feet. Soon as I pulled the cover from over his dick, that big mothafucka stood straight up, almost hitting me in the eye. I licked my lips then started playing in my pussy. Lowering my mouth down to his member, I began to take him in my mouth, slowly letting my saliva build up just the way he liked it. After deep-throating him like it was going out of style, I pulled back right before he was about to nut. I knew that would fuck with him, but oh well, he should have waited 'til he was at least fully healed.

"Dammit, woman. You know I hate when you do that shit. I be right fucking there and you hop up."

"Price you have to pay when you should be waiting for some pussy. Now lay your ass back so I can continue to please my man."

He didn't say sit else as I climbed on top of his long pole and began to ease on down his dick. I began to rock back and forth, slowly trying not to hurt him while giving him what he wants and what I needed. Shit after he got his nut and I get mine, I had some shit to tell him, and I didn't know how he would even react to this news. But let me focus on getting this nut while I'm playing. I continued to grind on his dick. I felt my nut rising, but I didn't stop I wanted to make sure he got his too.

"Awww fuck, ma! I'm 'bout to nut."

"Then cum with me, daddy. I'm right there with you, ride this wave with me. Baby, come on and ride this fucking wave. Shit! Yes, I'm cumming."

I released all down his pole as he coated my walls with his semen. What he didn't know just yet was that I am already eight weeks pregnant. Yes, you heard me right. I am pregnant; his ass got me good. He had to have got me when he first got out. Before he got out, I wasn't even fucking Cortez anymore and hadn't really been taking my birth control, but I still had some. So when Cornell came home, I started taking them again, but I guess they weren't effective because here I am two months pregnant with our baby, and I had to tell him. I just hope he won't think I trapped him. I didn't think about checking the dates on my pills.

Shit, my ass never thinks about shit like that, to tell you the truth. I hopped off his dick and went to the bathroom to wet a washcloth with some warm soapy water then washed my pussy and then grabbed another washcloth and wet it to wash his dick off. When I went back to the room, he was sleep, but he wasn't 'bout to sleep much longer 'cause we had some things to discuss. Like this baby is the most important thing that I need to talk to him about, everything else can wait. I washed his dick off, put my clothes on, covered his body back up, and went on to wake his ass up so we could talk about this baby.

"Cornell baby, you gotta wake up 'cause we have to talk. I have something I need to tell you."

"If it's bad news, it can wait. I'm tired. Shit, you took a lot outta me riding that wave, girl."

"I'm sorry to tell you, but this shit can't wait. We have to talk about this shit now."

"You get on my damn nerves with this shit. Always wanna talk when I'm trying to sleep. Damn, what is it, man.?

"You know what? Fuck it, I will just keep it to myself. I'm 'bout to go back to the room, shower and lay down. I ain't got time for your bullshit."

"Wait, ma, don't leave. I'm sorry I shouldn't have talked to you like that. I'm just sleepy, baby. Come here and give me a kiss. Let daddy make it up to you."

"Nah, I'm good. You can keep your kisses to yourself. I don't want them."

"Girl, if you don't bring yo ass over here, we gonna have a real big problem. Now come the fuck here." I walked over to him and sat in the chair next to the bed. Fiddling with my fingers, I looked down because I didn't know how to tell him we were having a baby.

Then I looked up at him. I was about to speak, but he spoke.

"So, what are you really mad about and don't lie to me either?"

"You brushing off what I have to tell you like it doesn't matter when this does matter. It's a life-changing decision for the both of us."

"What the fuck is so life-changing about what you have to tell me?"

"Look, it's no easy way to say this but I'm just gonna come right out and say this. We are having a baby. I found out like two weeks ago that I am pregnant. I'm eight weeks along and no, I didn't trap yo' ass. I started back taking my pills after the first time we fucked at the house. But I hadn't taken them in a while because I wasn't sleeping with your brother anymore since I found out he was fucking other bitches. So, if you gonna ask me if I'm sure that it's your baby, yes I am and don't ever disrespect me like that, nigga."

He looked up at me then started smiling like I didn't just say I was pregnant. He probably the one who trapped me. I looked at him shocked at how he was smiling at me.

"Ok, so why are you smiling like that? What did you do?"

"Well, I kinda did nut in you on purpose hoping to get you pregnant, but I didn't think you were since you didn't have any signs. But I guess I was wrong. I've been waiting on this day for so long."

Did this nigga just say he got me pregnant on purpose? I know he didn't just say that shit? I looked at him, shocked as fuck.

"Did you just say you were trying to get me pregnant?"

"Yes, I did. Is that a problem?"

"Well, it's not really a problem, but you could have said something. Instead I been sitting here worried that you were gonna think I trapped you."

"I would never think you trapped me, baby. I want to be with you for the rest of my life."

"Wait, what are you saying right now, baby?"

"I was gonna wait to do this when I had a ring, but hell right now is a good enough time then any, if I do say so myself. Give me your hand." I handed him my hand then he continued to talk. "Tonia baby, you came into my life when I had nothing or no one. I lost the first love of my life Stacee, and you were there to pick up the pieces from that. Who would have thought that meeting you in the club all those years ago would lead to you and me getting ready to have a baby and us falling in love with each other as we did? I know that we still have some things to work out, but baby, I love you. I want to spend the rest of my life loving you and making you the happiest woman in the world. Will you marry me and make me the happiest man in the world?"

"Oh my god! Baby, yes, I will marry you," I cried tears of joy.

"I know I don't have a ring yet, but when I get out this hospital, I'm going to get you a ring for damn sure."

"Awe baby, I understand. I know you just woke up from a coma, so with that being said. Get better first then you can go ring shopping and get my ring." I stood to my feet and leaned over him to kiss his lips.

"Now you get some sleep. I'ma go to the room, shower and change. Then I will be right back after I get us some food, do you want anything special?"

"Baby, bring me some Gates BBQ. I want a mixed plate with fries, baked beans, potato salad, and get one of them sweet potato pies too. Get me some lemonade too.

"Ok, I will be back in like an hour. Get some rest."

I walked over to the closet, grabbed my purse, kissed Cornell then walked out the room towards the elevator. As I got on the elevator, I just thought back to how this all came about and how happy Cornell makes me. I just wish I had someone to share this with. I was raised in the system, I don't know my parents; never even tried to find them. They didn't care to find me when I turned eighteen, so I wasn't going to do the same. If they wanted to find me, then they would find a way to do so. It just hurts sometimes that they never tried to find me. I mean, for heaven sakes, I'm their daughter. I couldn't be that parent that just gives up my child and not come back for them or even come looking for them to explain why I gave them up. But that's another topic for another day. I'd be going all day about that if I had to.

Getting off the elevator, I walked out of the hospital towards my car. Getting in my car, I drove by the shop to see how the renovations were coming along. It was two floors to my shop, so what I was doing was making the top floor the dance studio for pole dancing, and then the main floor will be for the tattoo shop. I loved dancing, so what better way to show my skills off then through pole dancing classes. Finding this place was a dream come true. I can do everything I ever dreamed of doing. I pulled up and got out the car to head inside. Looking around, I was amazed at how it was coming along. Walking upstairs, I looked at all the poles set up, and I was amazed at how my dream was coming to life.

Going back downstairs, I walked out and locked up then headed towards the hotel we were staying in I haven't had the chance to look for houses yet, but I was going to give my realtor a call tomorrow morning to get started on that for when my baby does get to come home. I would like him to come home to a new house and not a damn hotel room. Pulling up, I parked then went inside, showered and was headed right back out the door to go order this man's Gates BBQ he asked for. I ordered his food then waited for his food until it was ready then I headed right back to the hospital. I walked in with his food, and when I got to his room, this man was sitting up watching tv like I didn't tell him to rest 'til I get back.

"Didn't I tell you to rest 'til I got back with your food?"

"I did, but then these damn nurses and doctors came in to change my bandage and check my wound. So I have been up for like thirty minutes really. Plus, my ass hungry as fuck right now."

"Well, here is your food and drink. Eat up, babe, you gonna need it."

I sat his food on his dinner tray and pushed it over to the bed in front of him. That nigga opened that box and dug right on in. I, on the other hand, opened my food and started picking through it, but soon as I took that first bite of food, I was running to the bathroom throwing up. Damn, this baby was making me fucking miserable already. I couldn't eat or drink shit for the life of me.

"Baby, are you ok in there?"

I wiped my mouth then headed back out towards the room.

"I'm ok, babe. The baby just didn't agree with the food I got. I guess this lil' person inside here just wants to give me hell. Good thing this shit will be over within another month, they say."

"Awe, my poor baby giving you the blues I see."

I nodded my head then took a seat. I was mad that this little person was being so fucking hard-headed and not letting me eat shit.

"Baby, I will be right back. I'ma go get some soup and a sprite so I can at least put something on my stomach."

"Ok, baby, I ain't going anywhere anyway. Soon as I finish eating, I might just try and go back to sleep anyway cause yo' nigga is tired after that pussy and that meal you just got me."

I laughed at his stupid ass then walked back out the door to head to the cafeteria.

Chapter 12

Cortez

I've been sitting in this mental facility for some time now, waiting to find out when I could go home or if I was going to jail or whatever the case may be. I couldn't wait 'til the day I can be with my family again. My lawyer told that my brother survived and woke up last week. Sarah has been bringing my son to see me as well, so I don't miss anytime with him. He was a breath of fresh air because I hated being in this place with these people. I know that I needed it because the doctor that I have been seeing told me that I have a very serious case of Bipolar disorder. Which I already knew about, but I stopped taking my meds some years ago because I felt like I didn't need it. Plus, I didn't like the way they made me feel. When I was younger, I was on Seroquel, but now they have me on lithium. It has been helping me more than the Seroquel did. I do feel bad for everything I put my brother through. From him getting sent to jail and losing his fiancée Stacee. Then with me shooting him and almost killing him, I was starting to feel remorseful over it all.

Today I was sitting down in my room, writing down my feelings and thoughts before I had to go to one of the group sessions. But this one writing exercise I was working on was an apology letter to my brother for everything I put him through.

Cornell,

My brother, I know I have done some very bad things to you in the past five years, and I am writing you this letter to apologize to you and admit my wrongdoings. Five years ago, I was the one to send that officer after you that night. It wasn't supposed to go the way it did. He was only supposed to arrest you, not kill Stacee. I feel terrible that he killed her. She was supposed to be your wife, but that officer took her from you. I am very sorry for playing a role in her demise and you being sent away for five years.

Bro, I also want to apologize to you for shooting and almost killing you. I was only trying to scare you; I didn't think you would get out the car and start shooting back. Foolish of me, yes, I know. If you could please find it in your heart to forgive me for everything that I have done to you, I would never do anything like that again to you.

They tell me I have a very serious case of bipolar disorder that has been left untreated for some time now. I already knew I had it but stopped taking my meds because I didn't like how it made me feel. But I am now on a new medication that is working really well right now I just have to stay on top of it. I plan on taking these meds even if I am able to come home soon.

I want you to know that I love you, and I hold no more ill feelings towards you. I was dealing with a lot back then. Then finding out Dad wasn't really my dad is what really triggered things for me, and I took it out on you. And for that, I am sorry. I shouldn't have taken it out on you at all because it is not your fault. You didn't do any of this, and it was wrong of me to take it out on you. Thank you for everything that you have ever done for me. I hope that you make Tonia as happy as you made Stacee. She deserves it so much more than you know. You are all she has. She is not gonna tell you this, but I know that she hurts not knowing who her biological parents are, so a few years back, I went out my way to help find them.

They are in Atlanta, Georgia, married with kids. They would like to meet her if she is up for it. They said they have been looking for her since she was eighteen, but nobody knew how to find her. I will be sending my lawyer to the hospital today to give you the information you will need to get a hold to them. Please help her get to that point where she is ready to meet them. I love you, brother, and again, I am sorry for everything I have put you through.

Your little brother,

Cortez Bishop

After closing my notebook and putting my pencil on my dresser, I slipped on my Nike slides, grabbed my notebook up and then headed on out my room to line up for class since it was almost time for class. As I stepped in line, I noticed that one of the girls that were in here with me was looking really sad and depressed today. She was normally that bubbly, happy go lucky type of girl, but today she just didn't seem like herself. So I walked over towards where she was, tried to spark up a conversation and see what was bothering her.

"Hey, Risa. What's wrong, Ma? You don't seem like yourself today?"

"I just found out that my husband of eight years has filed for divorce and full custody of our kids because I'm in here. He says he didn't sign up for this shit here. I thought he loved me, but I guess he didn't love me enough."

"Look, Ma, if he wanna go, let that nigga go but fight for your kids, you hear me. That's his loss. You look to be an amazing woman, probably even a damn good mother and wife. So fuck him and keep pushing through and do what needs to be done for you to get out of here. I have a lawyer that can take your case. If you need it just let me know."

"Cortez, thank you so much, and yes, please get me that information. You just made my day for sure. You have come a long way since being brought here."

"Thank you, Risa. Now let's get in this class."

We both walked into our class and took our seats. Looking around the room, I noticed that a gentleman that was normally here at all the classes wasn't even in here today. Maybe he finally got to go home or he just wasn't feeling class today. The person that was conducting the class today was this nice young lady name, Ms. Danika Brown. She is married to the very infamous Jabril Brown. She told us a little about her and his story and how he helped her love again and took her daughter in as his own. She is a very cool chick.

"Good morning ladies and gentlemen I see some new faces in here today. Let me start by introducing myself to everyone that doesn't know who I am. My name is Danika Brown. I am gonna be your instructor for this class. I am married and have a child and also am due to be having my second child soon. My husband saved me and my child and also showed me how to love again. He is the reason why I decided to get involved with mental health patients. I am also an Rn nurse, but this here is my side hustle as y'all say.

I'm all about getting that bag for real, but I do like to help others. Now that you all know me, let's get to know one another. Who would like to start?"

I stood to my feet and introduced myself and told a little bit about me and what brought me here. Then everyone else followed behind me. The class was going so good today. I was actually proud of myself for even participating today because usually I just sit there and listen to everyone speak. So this was my first time even participating today. I think I was taking a big step in the right direction. An hour later, class was over, and I was headed back to my room to relax till it was time for the next class then lunch.

As I laid back in my bed, I looked up at the ceiling, just thinking about everything going on right now in my head. I want to be happy in my life, but I don't know what else could make me happy besides my label and son. I wasn't really in love with Sarah; she was just a thing to do since I wasn't taking my meds then. I knew she was Cornell's jump off when I started fucking with her, but I didn't care I just wanted some new pussy. And I got that out of her, but somewhere along the line, she fell in love and got pregnant with my son. So I couldn't cut things off with her as I should have a long time ago. Right now, I felt like I owed her an explanation and to give her, her freedom to be with who she wants when she wants.

I will still be there to help raise my son. We could be the best co-parents that there was. I just hope and pray that I don't break her heart and that she doesn't get too mad at me, then try and keep my son from me. I just want to be happy, and I want her to have the same as well. So I decided to get up out of my bed and go to the phone and make this call for her to come up and see me so we could talk alone. She could even take the baby over to my parent's house, and they will watch him while we have this talk.

Making my way to the phone, I took my seat in the chair in front of the phone, then picked it up and placed the phone call that I needed to make. The phone rang three times before she picked it up.

"Hello, Cortez. What's up? I'm really busy with the baby, what you need?"

"Well, I was calling you because I need to see you tonight for a visit. We have some things we should talk about alone. Take the baby to my parent's house to see if they will watch him so we can have a visit alone."

"Fine, Cortez, I will see what I can do. I'm glad you called because I feel like we need to talk too. it's been a long time coming anyway."

Hearing her say that I knew she must have been feeling the same way that I was feeling. But it didn't make me feel some type of way about it at all. We were wrong for doing what we did. It was time to make things right with everyone. I really did love Tonia when I started out with Sarah, but I got caught up in this jealousy shit with my brother. But now it was time for me to set the record straight and get everything off my chest now.

Hanging up with Sarah after saying our goodbyes. I looked up at the clock to see if I had enough time to call my parents to ask if they could watch my son so I could have this visit that is much needed for me and Sarah. I had a few minutes to spare, so I picked the phone back up and called my mom's phone. She answered on the second ring.

"Hey Ma, how are you doing?"

"Boy, I'm fine. How are you doing?"

"I'm doing much better then I was before, but that's not why I called you today. I want to ask you something if its ok with you?"

"Sure, go ahead and ask me, son."

"I was wondering if you could watch my son so I could have a visit with Sarah by ourselves so we could talk alone, please?"

"Sure, son, I would love to watch my grandson. Tell her to bring him by. I am here. I ain't going anywhere till later on this evening when I go see your brother."

"Thank you, mama."

"Your welcome, baby. Now let mama get off of here. I have to finish getting my house clean before that baby mother of yours brings the baby by here."

"Alright, mama. Love you and will talk to you later."

"Love you too, son. Bye."

We hung up the phone, then I got up and went to stand in line, waiting on the next class to start. As I stood in the line waiting for class to start, I looked around and noticed that Risa wasn't in line yet, so I walked off to go find out where she was at. I walked towards her room but didn't see her in the hallway anywhere, so I continued to her room 'til I got to the door, which was closed. I knocked on the door lightly just in case.

"Risa Ma, it's me, Cortez. It's time for our next group session." I waited a few minutes and still got nothing in response, so I knocked again. "Come on, girl, open up. I'ma stand out here 'til you open this door."

Still, there was no response, so I turned the doorknob, and it was unlocked. So I walked into the room, and she was laying on the bed sleeping soundly. I walked over to her bed and shook her lightly to wake her. She stirs in her sleep a little then opened her eyes. Looking up at me smiling, she sat up in the bed.

"What's up, Cortez did you need something?"

"No, but it's time for group, so come on. Let's go."

"Ok, here I come. I will meet you there."

"Aiight Ma, see you down there."

I turned and walked out of her room then went right back to the front to stand in line. When I got to the front where the line was, nobody was standing around, so I knew they were already in the area where the group was being held. When I walked inside, everyone looked up at me, but I didn't pay them any mind I went right to my seat. Soon as I took my seat, in walked Risa. She took her seat beside me, then the instructor got right down to it. She introduced herself, and then we all introduced ourselves once again. The class was going along great, but when I looked up at the clock, it was now time for the group to be over and time for lunch. So we were all excused to head out for lunch.

Walking out, we went to stand in another line. Yes, they had us lining up like we were kids in school whenever it was time for anything. I couldn't wait until I can go home. It was now time for us to head down the hall to the cafeteria so we could eat.

Some hours later...

I was sitting in my room relaxing, waiting on my visit with Sarah. It was time for visits, and I was just sitting around waiting on her to come on back. That way we can have this well-needed conversation that needed to be had. There was a knock on my door, so I looked up, and there stood Sarah looking nice as ever, but I wasn't on that right now though.

"Come on in, Ma."

She took a seat on the bed next to where my bed was. She looked kind of off, but I wasn't gonna let that stop me from what I needed to say. I had to get this shit off my chest and had to get it off my chest now before I lose my mind.

"Hey, Cortez. How are you doing?"

"I could be better if I could just go home, but I will live. Anyway, that's not why I called you here today. We need to talk about us."

"Ummm, ok. I think we do need to talk about us too."

"So look, I know we have been fucking around with each other for what a few years now, right?"

"That's correct."

"So I'ma start by saying thank you for giving me my son. Then I wanna say that I should have never started this thing with you. You were my brother's jump off, and that shouldn't have happened period. Not only were you his jump off, but I was engaged to Tonia, and I am still in love with her, but she doesn't want me that I get. But I can't be with you right now because I'm not in love with you and this here should have never happened. You feel me."

"I totally understand where you are coming from. I am not in love with you either. I am actually in love with your brother, but I know he doesn't want me but that he wants your ex-fiancée. I should have never gotten involved with you. But I did, and for that I'm sorry. I have decided today that I am giving you full custody of our son when you get out of here because I can't raise him. I never wanted to be a mother. I don't want to be held down. I want to be able to come and go as I please. Having a kid, I can't have that freedom that I want. Basically, what I'm saying is after today you won't see me anymore. Your son is with your mother. I took her some of his stuff that he will need to get by 'til you get out of here. But I won't be here in Kansas City anymore. I am leaving town tonight."

Wait what why are you doing this? You can't walk out on your son, girl. That's not fair to him."

"WELL, I DON'T WANT TO BE A MOTHER ANYMORE I CANT DO THIS SHIT. I HAVE TO LEAVE I NEED TO BE FREE FOR ONCE IN MY LIFE. IT'S TIME FOR ME TO SPREAD MY WINGS AND FLY AND DO WHAT I AM MEANT TO DO ON THIS EARTH. AND THAT IS NOT BEING ANYONE'S MOTHER. IM SORRY BUT I CAN'T DO THIS ANY LONGER. THANK YOU AND TAKE CARE OF OUR SON."

I looked up as she stood and walked out the room and out my life forever. I couldn't believe what she just said to me. Here it is, I thought she loved being a mother, but I guess she was putting on a front. What was I gonna tell my son when he notices that his mother isn't around? How do I explain to him that she didn't want to be a mother and walked out on us?

I don't know how I would do this, but I knew I would do it and take it on in strides if I had to. My son means the world to me, and I was going to make the

best of this and show him he is loved.

Chapter 13

Cornell

It was finally time for me to go home and I couldn't be more happier. I have been stuck in this hospital for far too long. Yesterday I had a visit from my lawyer, which turns out to be my brother's biological father and his attorney as well. He dropped off a letter and some other info from my brother. He actually admitted to everything he has done and more. Then he gave me the info I needed to find Tonia's parents. I was going to look into them when I got out of here to make sure they were indeed her parents. I wasn't just gonna pass her this info without not knowing if they were the real deal.

Climbing out the bed, I started to get dressed while waiting on Tonia to get here. As I pulled my jeans up around my waist, I looked up because there was a knock on the door. In walked my niggas, Red and Preston.

"What's up, my niggas? What y'all doing here?"

"We came to take your ass home. Your girl had some last-minute things to handle, so she sent us here to pick you up," Red stated.

"What the hell is that woman up to?"

"Shit, yo' guess is as good as mine," Preston replied.

"Well, let me get my shirt and shoes on, then we can head out after the nurse brings in my discharge papers. But check it. I need y'all to take me by the jeweler to get my baby's engagement ring. I wanna have it for her when I get there. That way, I can do this shit the right way and ask for her hand in marriage."

"Wait, what? You really asked her to marry you already?" Red asked.

"Hell yeah, nigga. I sure in the hell did. She is it for me, and she 'bout to have a nigga's kid too. But look, I want you to look into this info I got from my brother about her family. I need to make sure it is legit before

I pass it on to her. I don't want to get her hopes up, and this shit is fake, you feel me?"

"We got you, bro," Preston replied.

After getting my shirt on, there was another knock on the door. The my nurse walked with some papers in her hand that I was guessing had to be my discharge papers finally.

"Well, Mr. Bishop, looks like you are all set to go. All I need is your signature right here, and then we can get you on out of here. But I will tell you, I have to get the wheelchair and push you to your ride. It is the policy that you are wheeled out of here."

"That's fine, Janice. I understand. Let's get to it 'cause I'm ready to go home to my soon to be wife."

She handed me the clipboard with the paper on it to sign along with the pen. I signed it, then she walked out and came right back with the wheelchair. Preston went to get the car while Red stood there waiting along with us. I sat there, lost in my thoughts about everything. I was wondering if I could forgive my brother for everything that has happened in these last few years. I was really hoping that I found it in my heart to actually forgive him since Stacee did tell me that I should forgive him for it all.

I am gonna work on it, but its gonna take some time. Seeing Preston pull up, the nurse wheeled me over to the car and helped me get in. We peeled off towards our destination. We pulled up to the jeweler store, Preston parked, then we all hopped out the car to go inside to pick this ring out. As I walked around the store looking at all these nice ass rings, I just couldn't decide on which one I wanted to get her. So I enlisted on a female worker to help me pick the perfect ring out for my lady.

"Ayee, miss lady, can you help me over here please?"

"Sure, what can I help you with, sir?"

"I'm looking for an engagement ring for my girl."

"Oh, how sweet. What did you have in mind?"

"Well, that's where you come in at. I can't seem to make up my mind choosing between this one here, this one, and this one. I know she would like either or, but I want it to be perfect for her."

"Ok, so if it was me, I would go with the pink cut princess diamond ring. That one is my favorite."

"Ok, great. I will take it. Here is my card, go head and box that ring up for me. Please and thank you."

"Sure, no problem. I will be right back, sir."

She walked off, and I turned to the fellas, who were just standing around laughing it up and scrolling through their phones like some little bitches. So I walked over to them to see what was so funny right now.

"What y'all over here laughing about?"

"Shit nigga, we just scrolling through the book and came up across this nigga post saying that your brother old bitch Sarah is running around town in Texas saying she single and ready to fuck. Like the bitch ain't got a whole baby out here. Sad as fuck if you ask me, but that ain't my bitch. That's his shit. But what's funny about the shit is we all tried to warn his ass that she wasn't shit. She was only good for one thing, and that was to get that nut off when we were stressing or if we just wanted to bust a nut," Red stated.

"Man, I feel you. But damn, she just left her kid and didn't even wait 'til that nigga got out the mental place? That's fucked up; she could have at least waited. That bitch grimy for that shit. I'ma have to go check in on nephew when I get a chance. She probably dropped him off at Mama dukes house."

"You know that bitch did."

The store clerk walked over to us with my receipt and the ring box along with my card. I grabbed it all, thanked her then headed out the doors to go get back in the car so we can get to the crib. The ride to the crib was a silent one. We were all lost in our thoughts. Looking up, I noticed that we were pulling up to a nice ass mansion that I didn't know Tonia got for us. Not only that, it was cars all in front of the house. So when Preston pulled in the driveway, I hopped out the car. Walking inside the house, I looked around and noticed all my homies and my parents, even my nephew was here. Walking further into the house, I went to the kitchen, where I found my girl giving out orders to people. She looked up at me and smiled.

Then she ran to me and jumped in my arms just like I knew she would.

"Girl, you can't be jumping in my arms yet. You lucky I love yo' ass."

"I'm just so happy you are home, boo."

"Girl, you act like you didn't just see me this morning. Shut yo' lovesick ass up."

"Shut up, stupid."

She turned back around to finish what she was doing, but I turned her back towards me and kissed her so passionately then dropped down on one knee. I pulled the ring out of my pocket and began my speech to ask her for her hand in marriage. I handed my phone to Red to record for me so I can have that for my records.

"Baby, I know I asked you when I woke up to be my wife, but I wanted to do this the right way and get down on one knee with a proper proposal. You mean the world to me. You have changed my life so much in these last two years. I didn't think I ever would be able to get over the loss of Stacee, but you were there to pull me through, and I thank you for that. I want to spend forever with you, so I am asking you in front of all our friends and family today, will you be my wife?"

"Oh my god, baby! Yes! Yes, I will be your wife!"

She was looking around at everyone gathering around the kitchen with their phones out, recording our happiest moment. I placed the ring on her finger, got up off the floor, and kissed her sweet lips. I walked out of the kitchen into the living area and took a seat on the couch so I could rest for a little bit.

"Son, I'm so proud of you. You will be a great husband and father."

"Wait, you know about the baby, Pops?"

"Uhh, yea. Yo' mama can't hold water to save her life."

We laughed it up then I looked around to see all the ladies gathered around Tonia as she showed off her ring. I was loving how happy she was right now. Red walked over to me and let me know he hit his people up to look into what we talked about at the hospital and that they should be getting back to him asap. I nodded my head then looked over at my mother, who was enjoying herself. For the first time I could actually recall, she had a smile on her face. I was happy that I could witness this shit here.

"Pops, let me ask you something?"

"Sure, son. What is it?"

"Did Sarah leave Cortez's son with y'all and never come back for him?"

"Yeah, she did actually. She was supposed to come back and get him after her visit with your brother and never came back. Later that night, we got a call from your brother saying that she wasn't coming back and that she didn't want to be a mother. So she was giving him full custody and that we could keep him 'til he got out of the hospital or whatever. Why you ask me that, son?"

"Well, I heard she running around talking 'bout she single and ready to fuck and shit, so I had to find out what was what."

"This is gonna be hard on your brother, so we all will have to be there for him."

"Yeah, y'all can handle that I'm not there yet."

"That's fine, son. You will get there soon. Take it easy. Let me go get yo' mother's ass so we can head out. We just wanted to welcome you home."

My pops got up and headed to where my mother was, and they shared a kiss then headed out the door. Everyone else must have gotten the hint and started dipping out. I am glad they all came to show your boy some love, but I was ready to lay it down with my woman. I hadn't been able to hold her since I got shot. Now we were in our own home. Yes, God does answer prayers.

Getting up off the couch, I locked up then went back towards where my girl was so we could get up these stairs and go break this house in like it should be done. I was ready to blow her back out. If you know what I mean. That riding shit was for the birds.

"What are you doing, Cornell?"

"Come on, girl. It's time to break this place in."

"Boy, you stupid, but ok. Come on."

"Nah, you 'bout to sit on this counter and let me eat that pussy just like that, and you better not try and run either."

She laughed, but shit, I was serious as fuck. I put her ass on the counter, pulled her skirt up and her thongs to the side, then bent down and began to suck the soul outta her ass. That shit was wet as fuck already. It was glistening. She was squirming just like I knew she would.

"What I tell you? You better quit trying to run."

"Shit! Daddy, you making me cum and cum hard as fuck."

"Then let that shit go. Don't run from that shit."

I bent back down to get back to work. I started sucking on her clit then I took my finger and placed it at her opening, easing in her pussy just like I knew she liked. She was moaning and everything. I knew she was getting close to climaxing. She grabbed my head, pushing my face further into her pussy and started grinding against my face.

"Oh fuck! Yes, daddy, right there! I'm 'bout to cum and cum hard as fuck. Shit! Shit, yesss daddy! Yesss, nigga! Right fucking there, don't stop."

I don't know what got into her, but whatever it was, I was loving it. She was on one today. After she released, I stood to my feet, pulled her bottom half to the edge of the counter. I pulled my pants and boxers down, letting them drop to the floor. I rubbed the head of my dick at her entrance. That shit was soaking wet right now. I was just gonna tease her with the head, but that shit was calling for me to fuck the shit out of her. I plunged balls deep in that shit and went to work on her kitty. I don't know if I could hold my nut back by the way that shit was feeling, I was ready to let loose. I pulled out, trying to hold my nut. But as I pulled out, she pulled me back in. Grabbing my dick, she placed it back at her entrance. Pushing herself forward more, I couldn't control the feeling of her wet tunnel. Pregnant pussy is so amazing. I couldn't get enough of this good shit. She was going to have to take one for the team since I was about to let loose all up in her shit.

"Fuck, Ma! I'm 'bout to nut."

"Shit, me too. Cum with me, daddy."

Pumping in and out of her middle, I let loose. I felt her walls tightening up around my dick and her juices rain down all over my dick. Standing there for a few minutes as my dick pulsating inside her, I caught my breath then pulled out. Backing up to the counter behind me, I stood there relishing in the moment.

"Damn daddy, that shit was amazing. It feels good to be in our own place and to be engaged to the man that I am in love with."

"Baby girl, we in this for the long haul. Ain't no breaking up or none of that shit. If you get mad at me, we talk that shit out and no arguing. We got to think about our kid here too. I wanna raise him in a two-parent home. I love you, girl and I see us in this as a forever type of thing. I do have one thing to take care of later this week, but I want you to come with me though."

"Umm ok. What is it?"

"It's nothing bad. We just gonna go to the cemetery to see Stacee. It's something that I need to do. Can you ride out with me later to do that?"

"Of course, Baby. I got you."

Chapter 14

Tonia

Walking upstairs to the bathroom to go shower, I grabbed me a change of clothes and a towel, hopping in the shower. Drying off my body, I wrapped my towel around my body and walked out to the room. Cornell ass was laying across the bed, knocked out already. I lotioned my body down then got dressed. Nudging Cornell, he moved over to his side of the bed so I could get in the bed next to him. Laying in the bed as soon as my head hit that pillow, I was out.

The next morning...

Getting out the bed, I went to the bathroom to handle my hygiene. I was going to go cook us some breakfast. Hopefully, this baby will allow me to eat something at least for once. After brushing my teeth, I walked out the room, and Cornell was just waking up.

'Good morning, beautiful. How did you sleep?"

"Good morning, handsome. I actually slept well in your arms."

"Good. What you 'bout to do?"

"I'm 'bout to cook us some breakfast then get dressed. We have a doctor's appointment today."

"Ok, great. Let me hop my ass in this shower then."

He got out of bed and went to the bathroom. I lotioned my body down then put on my panties and bra. After that, I grabbed my robe, putting it on. I went to the kitchen to get started on breakfast. I grabbed bacon, biscuits, eggs, and some potato O'Brian's. Grabbing my skillets and a cooking sheet to put the biscuits on, preheated my oven, and began to cook breakfast. After I finished cooking, I set the plates on the table. Then I grabbed the orange juice out of the fridge, poured each of us a glass, and set them on the table.

"Cornell baby, breakfast is ready."

"Here I come, woman."

Taking a seat at the table, I waited on Cornell before I started eating. He walked in a few minutes later with just basketball shorts and a wife-beater with slides. I said a prayer over my food then dug in. After eating a few bites, my stomach started turning, so I jumped up to run to the bathroom. Soon as I got in the bathroom, I was throwing up in the toilet. This baby was really giving me hell. I can't wait 'til this last month is over because this shit is for the birds for real. Every time I eat something, this baby is making me throw up. That's why I was going to the doctor today so they can give me something for this morning sickness.

Going to my room, I went into the bathroom to brush my teeth again and then got dressed. As I was walking out the bathroom, Cornell was walking into the room.

"Baby, why you run off from eating?"

"This damn baby of yours won't let me eat shit for real."

He walked over to me then rubbed my hardened stomach. Trying to soothe my stomach, I guess. Then he bent down, kissing my stomach. After he kissed my stomach, he went to the closet to grab him some clothes. I walked over to my side of the closet, looking through the closet for something comfortable to wear. I decided on a red sundress, and some flip flops for the day. After getting dressed, I grabbed my purse and my phone, walking out the room. Cornell followed, and we both headed out of the house to my car.

Pulling off towards Research Medical Center to my appointment, we talked about when we would plan on getting married. I wasn't in a rush to get married right now. Since I'm pregnant, I didn't want to be fat and pregnant at my wedding. I am glad that I finally found the man for me; even though he is the brother of my ex-fiancée, but you can't help who you fall in love with. The heart wants what the heart wants.

Pulling up to the hospital, we both got out of the car and headed inside the office building. Walking inside, I looked around the office and noticed it was already packed. I just hoped it wasn't going to be an all-day thing. I still had to go by my shop to check on things. I want to be all hands-on with this. I checked in at the front desk then took my seat. As we sat there, I pulled my phone out to make a few calls while we waited. After making my phone calls, a nurse came out to call me back. Cornell and I got up and walked to the back of the office. The nurse had me pee in a cup, and then she checked my weight and my blood pressure. After going through all that, she started asking a few questions, basically family questions that I didn't know how to answer because I don't know my family. So I couldn't answer those. Maybe one day, I guess. After all the questions, she gave me a white sheet and told me to undress from the waist down but cover my bottom half up. She let me know the doctor would be in shortly.

Once she walked out of the room, I began to strip out my pants and panties. I sat on the table then covered my bottom half to just wait for the doctor to come in. there was a knock at the door then in walked a short lady who looked to be in her early 50s.

"Good morning Ms. Keys, how are we feeling today? My name is Dr. Jolie Lucas."

"I'm feeling fine now but every time I try and eat anything but soup I'm throwing it up. Is it supposed to be like this?"

"Everyone's pregnancy is different. Some don't have it at all, and some just have it in the morning, but then there are cases like yours where its everything you eat but certain foods. But lay back, and we will do a vaginal ultrasound to check the baby out and make sure everything is going ok."

That kinda made me feel better. I laid back on the table. She had me scoot down to the edge of the table, open my legs and place this dildo like thing that looked like it had a condom on it at my vagina opening and began the ultrasound by moving the doppler around. As she moved it around, I looked on and saw my little baby there looking like a little alien. Tears began to stream down my eyes. Cornell came over to me and wiped my eyes then kissed my forehead. Seeing my baby on that screen just did something to me. I was feeling over the moon right now.

"Ok, so the babies are fine. It looks like you are caring twins though. Let's see if we can hear their heartbeats today."

This nigga here wanted to cop a free feel of pussy and ass like we weren't in the damn doctor's office. I swatted his hands away then continued to get dressed. After dressing, we walked out of the room and went right to the lab to get this blood drawn. After getting my blood drawn, I walked back to the front lobby then made my next appointment.

We walked out the building hand in hand towards my car. Getting in, we drove back to the house so I could drop him off because he said he had a few things to go handle. After dropping him off to his car, I went by my tattoo shop/pole dancing studio to go see what was so damn urgent that they had to be blowing my damn phone up right now. I told them yesterday that I would be by today after my damn appointment.

Pulling up to the shop, I looked around but didn't notice anything out the ordinary, so I got out my car then went right on inside. But when I got inside, it looked like my business was broken into and vandalized. This shit just pissed me all the way off. Like how did somebody get here and do all this damn damage? I just don't get it. Why would someone do something like this to my shop?

I walked around the building, snapping pictures so that I could have proof of everything that has been done. Then I had to call the police to make a police report for my records as well. I told the guys that they could have the rest of the day off since it's nothing we could really do right now. I had to file an insurance claim to help restart everything up to fix all this shit that was destroyed. I didn't have money like that to just blow right now, so I had to play it smart and what better way to play it smart then to file the insurance claim since my business was broken into. Finishing with filing the claim, I locked up then left the shop to head home. This shit just ruined my day. I just wanted to go home, lay down, and try all over again tomorrow. Getting in the car, I sped all the way home. As soon as I got home, I ran in the house and stripped out of my clothes and went straight in the bed and cried myself to sleep.

Chapter 15

Cortez

It's been three months now since I been in this mental hospital getting my life together, and I am actually ready to go home, which I will be today. Thank God. I have missed being on the outside. My son needed me now more than ever since his mom walked out on us and never looked back. What she did was downright low, and I couldn't forgive that. So I had my father file for full custody while I was in here. My court date is coming up here soon.

I was packing my things up, getting ready to head out to the front so I could talk to the staff about my discharge, but before I left out, I had to stop by Risa's room. Me and her had become really good friends since the day she got word of her husband filing for divorce and full custody of their kids. My father is also working on her case, as well. I told him I would flip the bill for her case because I know she doesn't have it right now since she is in here. Now when she gets out of here, we will figure out where she would live. Now I know I am doing all this shit for her, but she needs to have someone in her corner right now. Her husband turning his back on her in this time was hella low. I wanted to be that friend she could turn to if she needed to. Knocking on her room door, I waited for an answer before I just walked in.

"Come in."

"Hey, beautiful. How are you doing today?"

"I actually feel good today. I just found out that I get to go home tomorrow, but there is only one thing that I am worried about, where would I live. But I will also need a job too, so I have to figure that out too."

"How about this, I have a house that I use to share with my ex-fiancée. Nobody is staying in at this moment in time. I haven't really decided what I wanted to with the house yet. Or I can get you a room if that would make you comfortable. It's all up to you, baby girl."

"I don't want to lean on you so much, Cortez. You have done so much for me already, and you don't even know me like that. I know you have your own stuff going on with your baby mama walking out on you and your son, I don't want to be anyone's burden."

"Look at me right quick. You are never gonna be a burden on me. We are friends and we are getting to know each other. If you can't tell by now, girl, I do like you and want to try a hand at a relationship, but only when we are ready for that. We will take things slow. That is slow as friends period. I'm not ready to jump into anything because I am still in love with my ex-fiancée, who is with my brother. But I need to work on me, and you need to work on you."

"When you say it like that, how can I resist, but look, you are right. I'm not ready for anything but friendship myself. I've been with my husband for so long and when I need help, he just up and says fuck it, I'm leaving her and taking our kids from her. That type of hurt can kill someone like me, but I'm going to push through, rise up, and show him what he will be missing out on. Thank you for being that shoulder to cry on and that friend that I need. I would like to stay in the house, but I have to have my own room. I will not be in a room with you. We will keep this thing between us friends until we both are ready for something more."

"Ok, great. That sounds like a plan to me. Let me head out here so I can get home to my son. Here is my number, call me, and I will pick you up tomorrow."

I leaned down, kissed her forehead then walked out the room to the front lobby where I was supposed to meet with everyone. I took a seat in the tv room and the nurse walked to go over my discharge papers. After going over my discharge papers, she cut my wrist band off and escorted me to the front of the building, where I was released to my mother, who had my son standing next to her. He ran up to me, and I picked him up. Kissing his forehead, I was excited that I was finally able to hold my lil' man. Getting in my mom's car, she drove me to my crib.

"Ma, how are Cornell and Tonia doing?"

"They are fine, son. Your brother is working through his issues. I think he will be coming around sooner then you may think. Just give him some time."

"Ok, I do miss the relationship me and him used to have. But also I am trying to get over them both being together. I know that I hurt her by cheating with Sarah and hiding my kid from her. I just have to get out of my head. Thank you for picking me up, Ma. I love you."

"I love you too, son. Now take that baby in the house and enjoy a little father-son bonding time. I will talk to you later."

I got out of the car, grabbed my son and went into the house. Walking around the house seemed so unreal that Tonia wasn't gonna be here anymore. It's just gonna take some time getting used to. I walked to one of the rooms to pick which room I was gonna set up for my son. I choose to have him right next to me. I had to order all brand new furniture; I didn't have anything for him here. I took him to the kitchen and sat him in the chair at the dining room table. Looking in the fridge, I looked to see what I had to cook for him. I didn't have anything for real, so I guess we were going shopping right now.

"Come on, son. Let's go get something to eat, eat."

"Yayy! Food, daddy."

Hearing him say Daddy just warmed my heart. I knew I could do this single dad thing. Picking him up, we walked out of the house and jumped in my car, going to Walmart. Driving down the highway, my music was on blast. Looking in the backseat, I saw my son bobbing his head to the music. This boy was bobbing his head to J Stalin. Pulling up to Walmart, I parked, grabbed my son from the back seat, and headed inside. I grabbed a cart, wiped it down, and put my son in the back of the cart. Pushing the cart around the store, I picked up everything I would need right now for my son. At least for the time being. I then walked around to grab all the groceries we would need.

I walked towards the front of the store to the check-out. As I was looking around the store checking out my surroundings, I noticed my brother and Tonia shopping for baby stuff. If I didn't know any better, I would say she was pregnant, but that couldn't be the case since she stayed taking her pills for birth control. I looked down at her stomach to make sure that she wasn't pregnant, but what I saw had me flabbergasted. I never thought that she would be having a baby by my brother so soon. Shit, we just ended things a little over three to four months ago. This was going to be hard now that I know she is pregnant. I turned back toward my son then pushed my cart up some more. I put my things on the little conveyer belt. Paying for my things, I rushed out of Walmart, hoping that they didn't see me.

After loading everything up in the car, I picked my son up, helped him in the car, got in and sped off towards my house. I couldn't believe this shit right here right now. I must have been speeding my ass off cause I arrived at my house within five minutes. Seeing them two just did something to my spirit. Getting out the car, I grabbed my son and as much stuff as I could to carry in the house. Unlocking the front door, I walked inside with my son following behind me, yelling out he was hungry. Shit, I know he was hungry, but he would have to wait 'cause I have to cook. I would just have to give him a little snack until dinner was ready. I set him in a chair at the table and handed him some crackers and fruit snacks. Then I went back outside, but when I got outside, my brother was standing against my car. I didn't know what this was about, but I hope and pray that he doesn't try and kill me. I have a son to live for.

"Bruh, please don't kill me. I got my lil' man inside and I am all he has right now."

"See, little brother, that's where you are wrong. You are not all he has. He has me, mom, your dad, and my dad. Yes, I know that pops isn't your real dad. Ma told me about him when I woke up from my coma. But that's not why I am here. I came here to tell you I forgive you for everything. It's taken me a while to even get up enough courage to even forgive you. But seeing you today at Walmart with your seed, I knew it was time to bury that hatchet. Look man, I just want my brother back; that's it, that's all. I need you, man. I know I broke code when I started fucking with your girl. I couldn't see past my revenge for Stacee, and for that I am sorry, but I love her. She is going to be my wife soon, and she is the mother of my seed. It's only right that I make her an honest woman."

"Bro, look, I miss you too, but right now, I need time to heal myself. I'm working on me right now, and that is more important, if you feel me. I know that we are brothers, and there is nothing that will change that. But right now, I just need my space to heal as well as get used to the idea that y'all are together, having a baby, and getting married."

"I understand. I will give you your space. You know where to find me if you ever need me. Much love."

He hopped in his car and peeled off. I went and grabbed the rest of the stuff out the car then went back into the house. When I walked into the kitchen, after taking his things to his room, I noticed that my son was sleeping at the table. I shook my head and took him to my room to lay him in my bed. Shutting the door, I walked back towards the kitchen and began to start our dinner. What I decided to make was baked BBQ chicken, mac and cheese and corn, along with some cornbread.

Hearing my son footsteps upstairs, I went to my room and grabbed him, then went back to the kitchen to put him in chair at the table. I made his plate and let it cool off before giving it to him. We ate dinner then retreated to the living room to watch some tv. I was so lonely in this house with just me and my son. I needed something to do. The ringing of my phone startled me. Looking down to see who it was, I noticed it was my father, Alvarez.

"What's good, Alvarez?"

"Son, I was just calling to check on you."

"I'm fine. Just sitting here relaxing with my kid."

"I will be by later on to discuss your case for full custody. We have to go over a few things before we go into court Friday."

"I will be here. I ain't got shit else to do right now 'til I find childcare for little man."

"I know a place that just opened up. If you need, I will shoot you that information."

"Yeah, yeah, do that please."

"Alright, son. I will be sending it over now. See you soon."

Hanging up the phone, I grabbed my son up then went to his room to see what all I had to do. I sat him down to his feet and he went right over to the toys to begin playing. While he was playing with his toys, I began to set up his bed I got for him. I got him the car's bed set with the toy box that goes with it. After setting up his room there was a knock at my front door. I looked out the window to see Alvarez, so I opened the door, letting him in. I showed him to the kitchen. Before I could sit with him though, I had to go check on my kid before I could settle down and have this conversation. Seeing that he was good playing with his toys, I went back down to the kitchen, where Alveraz was waiting for me.

"Ok Little man is straight, so let's get to it."

We sat there and discussed the strategy of what we would go for at court. By the time we were done, my son was running in the kitchen yelling cup. So I got up to get a cup, put some milk it then handed it to him. He sat right there on the kitchen floor, drinking from his cup. Alveraz got up to head out. We shook hands then he walked out of the house. Locking up, I went back into the kitchen to find Cortez Jr in there laying on the floor sleep. I swear this kid will go to sleep anywhere. Picking him up, I took him to his room, changed him into his pajamas, then laid him in his bed. I closed the door slightly, leaving it cracked a little so I could hear him just in case he woke up in the middle of the night. Walking into my room, I went to the bathroom, relieved myself then hopped in the shower. Letting the day's events wash over me and down the drain, I relaxed as much as I could right now. After standing under the water a few more minutes, I began to wash my ass. Getting out the shower, I dried off and walked out the bathroom to lotion my body down. After I grabbed a pair of briefs out my dresser, put them on, and climbed in bed. Soon as my head connected to the pillow, I was out like a light.

Chapter 16

Cornell

Today was the day we were finally able to find out what we were having. I was just hoping that the twins were healthy; I didn't care what the babies were as long as they are healthy. Yes, I would love to have a Junior, and I also would love to have a princess that I could spoil as well as her having me wrapped around her little finger. So I guess you can say I would love having the best of both worlds. Looking over at Tonia, she was rubbing her belly. I guess my kids were over there doing summersaults in her stomach right now, so I walked over to where she was standing looking in the mirror to rub her belly to get them to calm down a little bit.

Kissing her cheek as I rubbed her belly, I lowered my hand to her middle. I lifted her dress over her ass then let my finger do the talking for me. I know we supposed to be leaving out to head to the doctor, but looking at my pregnant fiancée had my dick on brick right now, so I had to climb up in that shit before we head out.

"Mmmhhh, daddy that feels so good. You gonna make me cum."

"Let that shit go then, Ma."

I undid my pants with one hand as I played with her middle with the other. Dropping my pants and briefs, I walked back to the bed backwards. Sitting on the bed, I turned Tonia around then pulled her thongs down to her ankles. She stepped out of them and climbed in my lap. As she eased down in my lap onto my already hard dick, I felt the heat radiating from her middle.

"Fuck, girl."

She began to rock back and forth slowly. I could feel her juices flowing down my shaft. She was getting ready to cum already, but I had to take control of this situation because I wanted to cum with her. So I flipped her over, putting her face down ass up. Spreading her pussy open, I put my dick at her opening and slammed into her middle. Taking her by surprise, I began to tear into her. She was throwing that ass back, matching me stroke for stroke. She was doing the damn thing. I thought I was taking over, but shit, she was taking over, and I couldn't control what happened next.

"Fuck, girl! I'm 'bout to cum."

"Shit me too, daddy."

We both released. Pulling my dick out, I rolled over and laid on the bed to catch my breath. After getting my breathing under control, I walked into the bathroom, grabbed a wash towel, and washed my dick with some warm soapy water. Walking back into the room, I went to pick my pants and shit up then put my clothes back on. Tonia was walking into the bathroom to handle herself. After getting dressed, she walked back out the bathroom, and we were now heading out of the house to go to this appointment. Getting in the car, I put my seatbelt on then sped off towards Research. Pulling up to research, we got out then headed inside the building. Tonia went to check-in at the front desk then took her seat. We waited about thirty minutes before a nurse called us back to the back. We went right on to the ultrasound room.

"Good morning Ms. Keys. How are we feeling today?"

"I've been great these two little ones are going crazy all day, but I have been feeling a lot better these days."

"That's great, so lift your shirt so we can take a look at these little ones."

She laid back, then the ultrasound began. Looking up at the screen, I saw my babies on the screen. I was so amazed I made these little creatures.

"Ok, baby A is being a little difficult. Let me see if I can get the baby to open its legs. Well, it does look like Baby A is a boy."

"I got my junior. Now, what about Baby B?"

"Baby B is a... Girl."

"Oh my God, we got the best of both worlds, babe," Tonia expressed.

"We sure in the hell do. I can't wait to meet these two. I'm actually going to be a father. I've wanted this for so long."

I was so excited to see that I was having me a little princess and a little prince. I never knew that I would be this excited about finding out the sex of my children, but I was. Looking on as the technician continued to move the doppler around Tonia's stomach as she looked at both babies and made measurements. After the technician finished looking over everything, she printed out a few copies of the ultrasound then handed them to Tonia.

After finishing up, we both walked out of the office to make her next appointment. After making her appointment today, we were going to go to the cemetery to speak my peace with Stacee. I know I was supposed to go when I first got out of the hospital, but I had to put it on the back burner for a minute. I wasn't ready to say goodbye then, but now I can go sit and say what needed to be said. Getting in the car, we both buckled up then I sped off towards the cemetery.

"Baby, I will give you your minute with her. Then you let me know when you are ready for me to come sit with you."

"Thank you, Ma. I appreciate you more than you know." I got out of the car then walked over to Stacee's grave. I took a seat next to her headstone then began to speak from the heart.

"Stacee honey, it's taken me a while to come up here to even speak my true feelings. Things have been hard for me since you were taken from me that night by that damn cop. He will be paying for what he did soon as I find his ass. I wish I could take back that night so much, but then I would never have met my now fiancée Tonia. She is everything to me. You would love her. I have brought her here with me today, but she is in the car giving me my time with you. I want you to know that Tonia and I are having twins, a boy and a girl." I stood up and walked over to get Tonia. I helped her out the car, then we walked over to the grave and took a seat.

"Stacee, this is Tonia, who I was just telling you about. She is having my babies. Tonia, this is Stacee. I was just telling her about our babies, and while I was telling her about the babies, I came up with a name for our princess."

"What name were you thinking about?"

"I was thinking about naming her Stacee Marie Bishop. Then lil' man, we can name him after me Cornell Bishop Jr."

"That sounds like a great idea, honey, but are you sure you are ready to name our daughter after Stacee?"

"I am very sure. I want to honor her and what better way to honor her then naming our daughter after her."

"Then that's a plan."

We talked for a little longer before I heard footsteps coming up from behind us. I turned around to see Cortez with his son walking up to the grave. He must have been coming to pay his respects as well. We had been getting along lately, and I was happy about that, but I would still catch him looking at Tonia like he was still in love with her. I wasn't going to hold that over his head right now. I know he was having a hard time getting over me and Tonia being together.

"Hey, Cortez. What you doing here? I didn't know you were coming here today," I asked.

"Yeah, I decided to bring Junior up here. I wanted to come and apologize for the part I paid in her being in this grave," Cortez confessed.

"Look, it's ok, man. I don't hold any more hard feelings towards you. I actually have let that part of my life go, that's why I'm here today," I stated.

"I understand, bro, but I haven't let that part go just yet. I still blame myself," Cortez replied.

"Don't beat yourself up about this. You didn't know that the officer you enlisted in taking me down was going to kill Stacee. That's not on you; that's on him."

While we were talking, Tonia grabbed Junior from Cortez to take him to the car while we talked. I really was appreciating her right now. She was taking care of a child that her ex-fiancée had on her while we talked.

"Look bro, you may not blame me for this shit, but I do its gonna take me some time to get over this shit."

"And I will be here for you every step of the way, but you have to let me be there for you. Don't push me away."

"I'm not trying to push you away. It's still hard for me to deal with you marrying my ex and having a baby with her."

"Look, you have to try to push that shit to the back of your mind. Live your life to the fullest and the best of your abilities. Besides, your niece and nephew need you around."

"Thanks, bro. Wait, you are having a son and a daughter? Congrats, man."

"Thanks, man."

We hugged it out, then I got up and walked away to give him his minute with her. I understand he needed his minute with her just like I needed mine. I wanted to give him his moment. Sitting in the car, I watched on as my brother sat there at the grave talking to Stacee.

Cortez walked back over towards my car, so I grabbed Junior to hand him to him. Getting out of the car, I handed over his son to him.

"You good, bro?"

"Yeah, I'm straight."

He walked off towards his car as I got inside mine to head home. Speeding off towards my home, I was lost in my thoughts about the conversation between me and my brother. He needed me right now and I had to be there for him. The shit that happened with Stacee is eating him alive. I had to do whatever I can at making him feel like it wasn't his fault, but how could I do that. Yes, he played a part in it, but it isn't on him, it's on that bitch ass cop that pulled that trigger.

"Cornell, are you ok, honey? You been quiet ever since we left the cemetery?"

"I'm good. I'm just tryna think about how I can help my brother. He is really down about this shit about Stacee. He is blaming himself something terrible."

"Look, I know he has blamed himself for these last few years, and he needs you right now, so be there for him and assure him that it's not his fault. Show him that you are there. Just keep doing what you are doing. He will be fine long as all of you are gathered around him, showing him you love him. Don't give up on him."

"I'm not giving up on him, Ma. I just can't let him go downhill again. I have to be there for him."

"And you will be there for him. While you are there for him, I will be there for you."

"Girl, I love your ass so much thank you for everything. I'm glad I found you."

"I love you too. Now let's get in this house. I'm hungry as fuck right now."

I laughed at her ass. She was always hungry these days. The twins were making her eat three times what she would. Getting out of the car, we walked inside the house. Going to the kitchen, I went to prepare something for lunch. After we ate then, Tonia laid down to take a nap. While she was napping, I was trying to plan a surprise baby shower. I wanted to do something special for her since she has been there for me so much lately. Its time to show her that I'm not taking her for granted.

Chapter 17

Tonia

I was now seven months pregnant. These babies were taking me through it. I was ready to have these babies like right now. I know it is too early for them to come out, but damn, I was ready to have my body back. Cornell and Cortez were getting along a lot more lately. Cornell let me know that Cortez wanted to sit down with me and get some things off his chest. So I guess today is the day that we are supposed to be having this conversation. Cornell was the one driving me to the meetup spot since I couldn't drive myself anywhere lately with this damn belly. Walking inside the restaurant that I was meeting Cortez, I looked around to see if he was here yet. When I saw him, I walked over to him to take a seat.

"Good afternoon, Tonia. How are you feeling?"

"Hey, Cortez. I feel fat and tired all the damn time."

"You look beautiful, not fat. But that's not why I called you here today. I wanna talk to you about everything that went down with us."

"Ok, but look, I don't want you doing this because you are trying to get me back or whatever. I love your brother and I'm happy with him."

"That's not what this is at all. I know you love him and that he makes you happy. I want to apologize for everything I put you through. I should have never cheated on you with Sarah. That was a mistake, but my son is not a mistake. Finding out about you and my brother took some time to get used to it. Yes, I still love you, but I have to let you go. I have since moved on with this girl I met name Risa. So today, I decided that it was time for me to let you go so I can fully move on with Risa as I should.

"Look, I forgive you, Cortez. If I didn't forgive you, then I wouldn't be able to give your brother the love that he so well deserves. He has been through so much since losing Stacee, and I want to be the one thing he can count on. With these two babies coming in just a short few months, we all need to be on the same page."

"You are right, Tonia. We do all need to be on the same page. My brother is strong, I know that, but I will be there for all of you."

This was a conversation that needed to be had. I got up from my seat but looked up to see Cornell coming my way with some chick I didn't know.

"Cornell, who is this woman?"

"Tonia, this is my girl Risa that I was telling you about," Cortez answered for Cornell.

"Oh, I'm sorry. I saw you two walking up, so I thought the worse."

"Look Ma, I will never cheat on you. You have to understand that I'm not that type. You and I are getting married and you are having my kids. That shit means a lot to me. you hear me."

"Yes, I hear you. I'm sorry again."

"Now sit down and let's eat."

Shaking my head at this nigga and his demands, we all took a seat. We ordered lunch then all sat around and talked, just enjoying ourselves. Who would have thought that we all would be sitting here with Cornell and Cortez getting along? Risa seems like a pretty cool chick; she is the right person for him. My stomach was starting to cramp up, but I know it couldn't be contractions; it was too early for these twins to come. I couldn't be in labor right now. Bending down in pain, I clenched my stomach. Breathing slowly, I tried to catch my breath as the cramp subsided.

"Baby, what's wrong?" Cornell asked.

"I think I'm having contractions?" I breathlessly replied.

"It's too soon. Let's get you to the hospital."

We all jumped up, and Cornell was so calm at getting me out the restaurant to the car. Getting in the car, Cornell ran around to the driver's side then hopped inside speed off towards the hospital. What could have been a twenty-minute drive turned into five minutes. Cornell jumped out of the car and ran into the hospital to get a doctor, I guess. When he came back, he had a nurse, and she was pushing a wheelchair. They helped me out the car and into the wheelchair.

"She can't be having the babies right now. It's too soon."

"We will do everything that we can to stop the labor."

"Please do whatever you have to do to stop this shit."

We headed up to labor and delivery. The nurse took me a room, gave me a gown, told me to change, and that she will be right back. After she walked out of the room, I looked up at Cornell, and he had this scared look on his face. I was scared too, but I had to keep it together, so I don't harm my babies.

There was a knock on the door, then the nurse walked inside. She hooked me up to the monitors. Then let me know that the doctor will be in here in just a minute.

"So, tell me what you were doing when you started having contractions?"

"I was eating lunch at a restaurant when the pain started. We were all having a good time."

"Ok, maybe it came from too much excitement or from what you ate or even just doing too much. Lay back and relax the doctor should be right with you."

After she walked out of the room, there was another knock on the door and in walked the doctor.

"Ms. Keys, it looks like someone wanted to make a grand entrance early, I see."

"I guess so, but it's too soon. Please don't let nothing happen to my babies."

Chapter 18

Cornell

"We are going to do everything we can to stop the labor."

I was praying that they were able to stop the contractions. Things have been going so well lately. This weekend was supposed to be the surprise baby shower. If the twins decided to come today, then we will have to put it off. Whenever it's time for them to come home, we will just do like a welcome home party, I guess, but I shouldn't be thinking about that right now. I need to be there for my fiancée.

"Argggg, shit! This shit hurts!!!"

Tonia started screaming. I know she was hurting, so I walked over to her to hold her hand and get her to calm down some. I wanted her to relax as much as possible.

"Tonia baby, relax and breathe for me. I'm here for you, Ma."

"I am fucking breathing. Don't come to me telling me to fucking relax and breathe when you don't know how this shit feels."

"Ms. Keys, relax. Let me take it a look at your cervix so I can check to see if you are dilated any."

The doctor went on to check her then we later found out that she was already dilated to three centimeters. If she was at three already, does that mean that they can't stop the labor or that they can? I had to ask for myself to know what was what.

"Doctor, does that mean that you can or you can't stop her labor?"

"Well, we will do everything we can do to stop her labor, but as of right now I don't think we will be able to. I'm sorry it's not what you were hoping for. They will be fine; babies can survive this early. We will also give you a medication to make sure the lungs of these babies are developed enough for them to survive on their own."

"Please do everything you can for our children."

The doctor nodded her head then walked out of the room. I sat there, rubbing her head to keep her calm. As her soon to be husband, it is my job to keep her calm. I was trying everything I could to keep her calm and relaxed, but nothing was working at this point.

"Baby, I will be right back. I'm going to step out and call my parents to get them here. While I'm out there, I will give Cortez an update since he just texted me to let me know he was here with Risa."

"Hurry back, please. I'm scared. I don't want to lose our babies. Don't let them die, please."

"They are not gonna die, you hear me? They will be fine."

She nodded her head, and I walked out of the room to make my call to my parents. As I walked down the hallway, I saw Cortez and my parents sitting there already.

"Mom, Pops, how did you know?"

"Your brother called us when he was on the way here. How is she?"

"Well, she is in labor. They say she is dilated to three centimeters, but they don't know if they will be able to stop the labor. She is scared right now and is going off on me when I told her to relax and breathe."

"Son, let me go in there with her. You stay right here with your father and brother. I will be back to let you know what is what. You stay right here and don't move."

I nodded and I walked with her to show her to the room. Walking back towards the waiting room, I sat down next to my brother and father. I was worried as hell about my twins.

"Where Risa at?"

"I took her home. She said she will watch Jr while we all are here."

"She seems like a good woman. Got her head on her shoulders straight. Does she have kids?"

"Yeah, she does. She is in the middle of a divorce and custody battle."

"Just keep your head on straight and be there for her."

He nodded his head, and I got up to go see what was going on, but when I got to the room, I heard Tonia screaming. So I ran in there to see what was going on, but when I walked in, she was bending over in pain on the edge of the bed while an anesthesiologist was behind her, putting a needle in her back. I'm guessing that was the pain medicine she had to been talking about. I know we talked about it, but I didn't know that it was a needle in the back. I walked over to her. I kissed her cheeks as she looked up at me crying.

"I'm not ready for this. I can't have them yet."

"Well, baby, we don't have a choice. Now, do we?"

"No, we don't have a choice."

"So relax, take a deep breath. We are gonna do this together. I'm here with you every step of the way."

It was all becoming so real. My babies were on the way, and there was nothing I could do to stop it. The doctors tried to give her the medicine to stop the labor, but it just didn't work. So we would be welcoming Stacee and Cornell Jr into the world in a few hours or more. Another nurse walked into the room, letting us know she was giving her medicine to help with the twin's lung's development to give them a chance at survival. Things were moving along real fast. The doctor was now back in the room, checking her cervix again since they couldn't stop her contractions.

"Ms. Keys, you are fully effaced and fully dilated. On your next contraction, I want you to push."

Tonia nodded her head. I stood next to her holding her hand. When she squeezed my hand real hard, I looked at her and knew she was having another contraction.

"Arghhhh! Make it stop."

"Push! 1...2...3...4...5...6...7...8...9...10... now breathe."

I looked down and I saw hair coming out. I saw the head slid out then the rest of the body slip out. I cut the umbilical cord. I was now the father of a little boy. Welcome to the world Cornell Bishop Jr.

"It's time to push Baby B out."

"Argghhhh!"

"Push! 1...2...3...4...5...6...7...8...9...10... now breathe."

As she was going through the second round of pushing, she was getting tired, but she had to keep pushing through. When it was time to push again, she was beginning to squeeze my hand hard as hell. Then I saw the baby slide out. It's a girl, welcome to the world, Stacee Marie Bishop. Cornell weighed in at one pound three ounces and Stacee weighed two pounds two ounces. They were a little underweight, but my babies are fighters. They are going to be ok; I just knew they would.

The nurse brought over the babies to show Tonia and me. She began to cry as she looked at our kids. Looking at my babies made this all feel so real. The nurse put the babies in the incubator and pushed the babies out of the room. I looked into Tonia's eyes, and she looked like she was urging me to go after the twins.

"Fine, I will go with them, woman. I will be right there with them every step of the way."

I walked out of the room and followed behind the nurses.

Chapter 19

Tonia

It has been a long day. I was laying in bed relaxing after giving birth to my son and daughter two months early. I was tired and worn out. I was also over the moon that I was now a mother and that they are ok. They may have a long recovery, but they were here, and they are fighters. Cornell was in the NICU with them now making sure everything was going right with them. I couldn't believe I am a mother now. I was going to do everything possible to protect them. After having my kids, it made me think that it was time for me to find my birth parents I've been putting it off since my first appointment after finding out I was pregnant, but I think I deserve to know who they are and why they gave me up. I needed answers. I was going to talk to Cornell about finding them.

The next day...

Today I was getting out of this bed and going to the NICU to see my kids. I was waiting for the nurse to come in with my wheelchair to take me down to go see my kids. I couldn't wait. I haven't been able to go down there since having them. There was a knock on the door and in walked the nurse pushing the wheelchair. She helped me out the bed and into the wheelchair. Cornell came walking in, looking happy to see me. He walked over and kissed my forehead. Then we all walked out towards the NICU. When getting in, we had to wash our hands and place a yellow gown on. After getting set up, I was able to go inside to see my kids. When I was finally able to see them, my heart broke seeing all these machines and tubes hooked up to my kids.

"Oh my God, my babies," I cried.

"They are fighters, Ma."

"I know, babe. It's just hard seeing them like this."

"Trust me I know it's hard."

We sat here with the kids just sitting there watching them. I wanted to just hold them and let them know that it's ok and that I am with them. I wanted to have a conversation with Cornell about finding my parents so while we sit here with our babies, I decided to just get this conversation out of the way now while it's still fresh on my brain.

"Cornell baby, I have something I want to talk to you about what's been on my mind since. Well, really since finding out I was pregnant. I've been thinking about finding my birth parents. Now that I have them, I owe it to myself to find them and get answers on why they gave me up."

"I'm glad you brought that up. When I woke up from the coma, Cortez had his lawyer/Pops bring over some information to me that I had looked into to see if these people were the real deal. So with that being said, Cortez found your birth family; they live in Atlanta and want to see you. I think you should give them a shot in explaining what went down when they gave you up."

"Oh my God, I do love you, baby. Thank you so much. Tell Cortez thank you for me."

"So what I will do is call your parents and fly them out here to see you if you would like."

"Yes please, baby. I need this closure in life."

He nodded his head. I was getting tired, so I asked him to take me back to my room. Getting in my bed, I laid back and went to sleep. As I slept, I thought about how my life is about to change with being a mother. I was happy that and I was going to meet my birth mother and father to get the answers I so desperately need.

A few hours later, I was now up. The nurse brought in a tray of food. I really wasn't hungry, but I had to keep my strength up. I had a plan to breastfeed my kids, so I was pumping, but they were being fed through a feeding tube until they can feed on their own. It was hard not being able to feed my kids, but I know that they will get there eventually. There was a knock at the door, in walked Cortez and his girlfriend Risa.

"Hey, Cortez and Risa. What y'all doing here?"

"We came to check in on you and see how the kids are doing," Cortez replied.

"I'm doing great and they are doing great too. They are fighting, that's all I can say right now. I know they will be fine."

"That's great, I am happy. They are good. I am saying a prayer for them and you," Risa stated.

"Thank you, Risa. Cortez, Cornell told me that you found my birth parents. I told him to thank you for me. I'm sure he already did, but I should thank you myself, so thank you," I stated.

"No thanks needed, Ma."

We sat around and talked for a few more minutes before I took them down to the NICU to see the kids. When we walked in, the nurse was just walking out the room.

"Oh, hey. Ms. Keys, you're back already? The babies are doing fine; they are true fighters. Dad just left out about fifteen minutes ago."

"Yes, I can't just sit in bed knowing they are in here fighting for their lives. I have to be with them as long as I can."

"I understand. I would do the same thing if it was my baby."

She walked out, leaving us alone with the babies. As I sat there with my babies, I was overjoyed even being able to see them at all. It could have been worse. I could be planning two funerals, but I'm sitting here watching my kids fight. We sat with the twins talking for a few more minutes then we went back to my room. When we got to my room, there was Cornell along with his parents, as well as two other people I didn't recognize.

"Cornell baby, who are these people with you?"

"Baby, they are your birth parents. They came down to see you."

"Hi, Tonia. I am your birth mother Tina. And this is your father Tony."

"It's nice to finally meet you two, but I do need to know why did you give me up?"

"When we gave you up, we couldn't give you the life that you deserved. We were both addicted to drugs. You were born a crack baby. I was still using when I was pregnant; I had to get my life together. The hospital called DCFS, and you were placed in DCFS custody. I went into rehab right after you were taken. I apologize for not being strong enough for you," Tina replied.

"The day they took you was an eye-opener for both of us. I should have been gotten my shit together. It shouldn't have taken me getting my shit together for you to be taken from us, sweetheart, and I apologize for that," Tony stated.

"Thank you for giving me that. I'm glad that you both got your stuff together, but why didn't you come for me?"

"We tried to find you for so many years, but we kept getting the runaround. Then they told us we didn't have the rights because our parental rights were terminated a year after you were placed in the system," Tina replied.

"They told us we had to wait for you to come for us or when you became of age," Tony stated.

"All this time I thought you didn't want me when in fact you did want me. This was all just the states doing. Thank you both for everything. If it's possible, I would like to build a relationship with you."

"Yes, we would love that very much. I have been dreaming of this day for so long. I know it will take some time to open up, but we will go at your pace," Tina replied.

I finally got the closure that I needed, which was much needed. I was ready to move on with my life now that I got closure. I was happy for once in my life. I had my twins fighting for their life. I had my soon to be husband and his family then I now have my parents. My life was amazing. I couldn't wait to be able to go home with my kids.

Chapter 20

Cornell

Today was the day that the twins were finally coming home. It's been a long four months, but it was well worth it for this moment. Today I was having a welcome home party for the twins. We never got to have the baby shower that we deserved, since Jr and Stacee decided they were going to make their grand entrance early. Tonia didn't know about the surprise welcome home party. She was at the hospital, getting the kids ready to come home while I get the house ready. I was going to meet her at the hospital in a short few hours.

I just got done hanging up the banners for the party. My parents and Tonia's parents were also here helping me get everything together. My mother and Tonia's mother were in charge of the food and drinks. Us men were hanging up decorations. I went into the twin's room to make sure that I have everything set up the way that Tonia decided she wanted. One side was painted in pink, the other side blue and I had a crib set up on each side of the room. I had Minnie Mouse everything on Stacee's side of the room and Mickey Mouse on Cornell's side.

It was now time for me to go pick up my family. So I headed out the door to go pick them up. Getting in my car, I sped off towards the hospital. I walked inside the hospital and went right upstairs to the nursery. When I got upstairs to the room, Tonia was feeding Stacee. I walked over to them and kissed both of them. Then I walked over to the bassinet that my son was in and picked him up. I smelled his head then kissed his forehead, placing him in his car seat. After Tonia was done feeding Stacee, she placed her in her car seat. The nurse came into the room with the discharge papers in hand, along with a wheelchair. I don't know what the wheelchair was for since Tonia isn't the one being released.

"What's the wheelchair for?"

"It's policy."

"Oh ok."

"So, are we ready to get these little ones out of this hospital or what?" Tonia replied.

"Yes, let's take our kids home, Ma."

Tonia signed the discharge papers, and then we were now on our way out of the hospital with our kids. The nurse and Tonia stayed at the entrance with the kids while I went to get the car and pulled up to the front. I got out to open the door for them. The nurse had one of the car seats in her hand, wheeling Tonia out. I took the car seat from the nurse and placed the car seat in the car as Tonia put the other baby in the car. We were now headed to the house.

"Baby, can you believe it we are finally taking our kids home?"

"Ma, I am over the moon right now. I can't wait to get you guys home, and our family is complete."

When we pulled up to the house, I opened the door for Tonia to get out, grabbed one twin, and she grabbed the other.

"Where are all these cars coming from Cornell?"

"I don't know, babe."

We walked inside the house.

"Surprise!! Welcome home!" everyone yelled.

I looked over at Tonia, who was now crying tears of joy seeing our whole family here. Her parents have now moved down here to Kansas City with their other two kids. Tonia didn't know that yet either. We were surprising her with the information today.

"Oh my God baby you did this didn't you."

"Yes, I wanted to surprise you and do something special for you since we didn't get to have a baby shower."

Everyone walked up to us, said their hellos and told us how cute our kids were. Looking around at our whole family let me know that what I was about to do was for the right reasons. What I'm saying is tonight I was going after that officer that put me in jail and killed Stacee. See, my brother let me know that he told the officer to get out of town, but he knows where he is hiding. I was going after him tonight after I get my family settled.

Tonia didn't know what I was doing tonight, and I wanted to keep it that way. Everyone was having fun, but it was starting to get late, so it was time for things to wind down.

"It's time for everyone to go home. The kids and my wife need to rest. Everyone can come back another day or tomorrow."

Tina was helping Tonia put the twins down while I made sure everyone headed home. Tina and Tony were going to stay with Tonia while I made this run. After everyone left, I went upstairs to check on Tonia and the twins. As I went upstairs to the twin's room, I saw that Tonia was in the rocking chair sleep. So I picked her up and carried her to the bedroom. I put her in the bed, covered her up, and kissed her cheek. As I walked downstairs, I noticed that Tina and Tony were sitting on the couch watching tv. I let them know I would be back tomorrow morning. I got in my car. Speeding off, I got to my destination in no time. I walked inside the little house they were hiding out in. Creeping around the house to check my surroundings, there was no one here right now. They must have been out. So since nobody was here yet, I decided to wait around until they came back. Picking up my phone, I made a call to Red to see where they were at.

"What's up, Bro?"

"Where are they now?"

"Right now he is inside the gas station. We are headed back to the spot."

"Ok, let me know when you are outside."

"Got it, bruh."

Hanging up the phone, I sat around to wait. After waiting for a few more minutes, my phone went off. I didn't even look at it because I knew it was Red letting me know they were here. Standing up, I moved behind the door, so they wouldn't see me when they came in.

"I'm saying, Jeremy, I want to go back home. We have been here for too damn long. And you still haven't explained why we had to up and leave everything. I need to go back home, baby I'm tired of living here."

"Look, we can't go back right now. It's not safe, honey. Now go put the kids to bed. I will be in there in a minute."

I let the wife and kids go before I announced myself to him.

"Well, well, look what we have here. If it isn't Officer Jeremy, I've been looking for you since I got out. You killed my fiancée and got me locked up for five years."

"M-man, how did you find me?"

"Don't worry about all that. Let's take a seat and chop it up."

We took a seat, and I pulled my gun out, sitting it on my lap just in case he got any bright ideas. Red and Preston walked into the house. Preston stayed by the door, and Red stood by the stairs watching to see if the wife and kid came back down the stairs.

"Officer Jeremy, you killed my fiancée, and you are going to pay for that shit. You may have got off with the Police Department, but you ain't getting off on that shit with me. So tell me why you did it?"

"That black bitch should have stayed away. It ain't my fault you called that bitch, and she came to your fucking rescue."

Hearing the way he talked about Stacee pissed me off, but I had to hold it together and not think with my emotions right now.

"That *black bitch* that you are talking about was my fiancée. She didn't deserve to die the way that she did by the hands of your racist ass."

"Fuck that bitch. I'm glad she is dead."

"You got a lot of mouth for someone that is about to die tonight."

"You may think your black ass is going to kill me tonight, but it may go the other way around. See, I've knew your little hence men were following me all day, so I let some of my friends with the police department know that you were coming after me. So if anything happens to me, you will be the first person they look at."

"But who said I was going to be the one to do it. You are going to kill yourself, and you are going to write a note stating why you committed suicide. So here you go, write what I tell you to write."

"Fuck no! I ain't writing shit."

Picking up my gun, I nodded my head at Red. Red walked upstairs then came back down with Jeremy's wife blindfolded and hands tied.

"So Jeremy, are you gonna write that letter or do I have to kill your wife?"

"Leave her out of this, man. She has nothing to do with this man come on Cor-"

"Don't you dare say my muthafucking name! You ain't slick."

"Man, come on."

"Now get to writing or I'm shooting your wife."

"Ok. Ok, man, you got it."

He picked up the paper and pen. I told him what I wanted him to write and he wrote every word. I knew he was gonna be on some shit when we got here, that's why I had Red and Preston with me. We used his wife as an incentive to get him to do what we wanted him to do. I am not one to hurt women and children. To me, women and children are off the table. That was a no go for me. I didn't want anyone going after my wife and children, so I wasn't going to do the same to someone else. I nodded my head to Red, and he pushed the wife back upstairs. He was to sit with her 'til this was all over. I set my gun down in my lap because my phone rang. Looking down to see who it was, I saw Tonia calling me. I knew this would happen. Shit! I should have told her I was stepping out, but she was sleeping so peacefully. I couldn't let that distract me right now though. I had to get my revenge on this punk ass cop.

"I see your little wifey is calling you. You better answer that phone call, bitch."

"Fuck you, she good. Don't worry about mine."

"You might want to get that."

Looking down, I saw she was calling back again, so I picked it up.

"Babe, what's wrong? Why are you calling me back to back, ma?"

"Where are you, Cornell!?" she cried.

"Baby, what's wrong? Why are you crying?"

"Cornell, I got up to check on the babies, and when I went into their room, they weren't in there. So I walked around the house to see if you or my parents had them, but you were gone, and my parents were in the guest room sleep, but they babies wasn't in there either."

"Wait, what the fuck you mean the babies weren't in their rooms?"

"Just what the fuck I said. They weren't in there, do you have them with you?"

"No, I ain't got them. I wouldn't take them out without letting you know. I'm on it though. Let me call you right back. Don't open the door for anybody unless I tell you too."

I hung up the phone, got up out my seat, and walked over to this bitch nigga. He was going to tell me where the fuck my kids was NOW. I know I said women and kids were out, but this motherfucka touched my kids, and he was about to see what it's like to mess with C-Note now. Preston locked the door, went upstairs and grabbed both this nigga's kids. When he came back down, the kids were blindfolded and hands tied up.

"Man, what the fuck you doing with my kids."

"See, you had someone come in and take my kids out of my home. So if you don't tell me where my kids is I'm going to kill both your kids right here in front of you. I will make it look like you fucking killed them then offed yourself. Leaving your wife to grieve the loss of not only her husband but her kids as well."

"M-man, come on. You ain't got to do this. I will tell you where they are. Just leave my kids out of it."

"You should have thought about that before you touched my kids."

"OK! Ok, they are with my wife's brother at his house."

"What's the fucking address?"

He rattled off the address and I sent it to one of my other guys and told them to go get my kids from that address. He knew he was to take out the mothafucka in that house and then get my kids.

Preston took the kids back upstairs. Now it was time to end this nigga's life. He has done too much to me, and he is wasting space on this earth. Seeing a flash of light, I looked up to car lights pulling into the driveway. So I walked behind the door and motioned for Mr. Officer Jeremey to come to the door. I held my gun up as he walked to the door. He opened the door, and my brother walked inside the house. I didn't know what he was doing here, but I didn't need him here involved with this shit.

"What are you doing here?" I asked.

"I couldn't let you do this alone, man. I had to be with you and make sure everything goes the way that it should."

"Well, I got one of my guys going to get my kids from his wife's brother's house. This muthafucking had someone kidnap my babies, man."

"WHAT!"

"You heard me. Right now get yo' ass in this house or get the fuck outta here."

He walked inside the house as I pointed my gun at Jeremey's head to make him move back to where he had been sitting at.

"Now, where were we? Ah yes, you are about to kill yo' self."

"Please, I don't want to die."

"Should have thought about that before you killed my fiancée then had me sent to jail."

"Man, come on, you ain't got to do this. I will tell them I killed her because she was there and I knew it would hurt you. Come on, please. I don't want to die."

"Too fucking late. Now hold the gun to your head and pull the fucking trigger."

He began to cry as I put the gun to his head and he placed his hand on the gun. His crying did nothing to me right now. He should have thought about that before he killed Stacee. He still hadn't pulled the trigger, so I looked down and spoke through gritted teeth.

"You better pull that fucking trigger. Right fucking now."

I pulled one of my other guns out since he thought I was playing with him, but what he did next, I wasn't expecting at all. He turned the gun on my brother.

"Woah, man. What the fuck are you doing?"

"You set me up. You didn't think you were getting out of here alive, did you?"

"Nigga, I am leaving here alive, so what you mean? You think I wouldn't come prepared for this shit."

He pulled up his shirt flashing his bulletproof vest and his gun. He pulled his gun, pointing directly at this nigga. I was going to let my brother handle this nigga if need be, but this nigga was taking his life or we were taking his life ourselves. We live this shit every day and have been living this shit for as long as we remember, so we know that this life we live could lead us in one of two places. Either in jail or dead. I've been to jail, and I'm not going back, but I ain't getting killed today. I know that much. We all were holding our guns on each other.

Boom... boom... boom...

Three shots rang out as we each let off a shot. But who was hit?

To be continued....

Stay tuned for the next part to see who was shot. Was it Cornell? Or was it Cortez? Or may, just maybe, it was Officer Jeremey who got shot?

Thank you for reading about the Bishops.

Please leave a review once you have finished. There will be a contest posted. Once you have posted your review, screenshot, and send me your proof of

purchase and review.

Thank you again for reading about these brothers.

About the Author

Author Shortee was born Jennifer Clark, she is a 37-year-old wife and mother of 3 from Kansas City. Writing has always been her passion. One day she decided to step out on faith and try her hand in this writing thing. She has 2 novellas. *Hood Lovin': Santa Sent Me a Boss and Baby Be Mine: Lovin' on My Boss*, 1 anthology *Makeup Won't Cover the Pain: A Domestic Violence Anthology,* and now she has a new series *The Bishop Brothers: In love with the Same Girl.*

Stay tuned for more to come from Author Shortee.

Follow her on Facebook: "Jennifer Holliman"

Go like her author page: Author shortee.

Instagram @Shortee302

Twitter "@shortee1982"

SNAPCHAT "Shortee3082"

To keep updated on what's next from Author Shortee.

Cover reveals, and contest will be held in my author group: Lovely Ann's Army. So If you haven't already, come to join us. We will be holding a discussion about this book in a week, so come join us.

TYANNA PRESENTS
Black Girl Magic
ARE YOU CURRENTLY LOOKING FOR A PUBLISHER?
TYANNA PRESENTS JUST MIGHT BE THE PLACE FOR YOU!
WE ARE NOW ACCEPTING SUBMISSIONS
IN THE FOLLOWING GENRES:
*Urban Fiction *African American Romance * Street Lit
*Women's Fiction *Suspense/Thriller
*BWWM *Erotica
IF YOU HAVE FINISHED MANUSCRIPT THAT YOU WOULD LIKE
TO SUBMIT FOR CONSIDERATION, EMAIL:
*Contact Info *Synopsis *First 3 Chapters
Tyannapresents1@gmail.com
SUBMIT TODAY!